A Breach of Trust

A BREACH of TRUST

JOHN DEAN

ROBERT HALE · LONDON

ISBN 978-0-7198-1431-0

Robert Hale Limited
Clerkenwell House
Clerkenwell Green
London EC1R 0HT

www.halebooks.com

2 4 6 8 10 9 7 5 3 1

Typeset in New Century Schoolbook
Printed in Great Britain by Berforts Information Press Ltd

Chapter One

D ENNIS SMART WALKED across the landing and hesitated at the top of the staircase, his heart pounding in his ears, his hand clammy as it gripped the banister. He knew instinctively, knew without even knowing how, that he was not alone in the house. Realized with a sick feeling that this was the moment he had expected, the moment he had dreaded. A man could only hide from the consequences of his actions for so long. He knew that; and in his sixty-five years, Dennis Smart had done plenty of things from which to hide. None worse than this, though, none so wicked. Not normally a man prone to fear, he felt cold as he stood at the top of the stairs.

Standing and looking down at the wood-panelled hallway, the manifestation of an opulent lifestyle financed by a ruthless business career, Smart tried to retain his composure. He peered in vain for movement in the half-light, strained to hear any sound which would identify the location of the intruder. Something that would give him the edge. Nothing stirred and he stood for the best part of a minute listening to the settling of the old house's timbers, the ticking of the grandfather clock in the hall, the.... When it came, the noise was behind him.

'Of course,' Smart murmured, without looking back.

He tensed as he heard the creaking of someone walking slowly across the landing towards him. Then the breathing. Close. Heavy. Familiar from his nightmares. Afraid to confront his killer, Smart continued to stare down into the hallway as if fascinated by something on the classically tiled floor.

'Don't turn round,' said a voice he knew well.

'Why?' Smart tried to sound calm although his trembling voice betrayed him. 'You scared to face me?'

'Me, scared?' A catch in the voice, a quiver of emotion, a sign of vulnerability. 'You're the one who should be scared after what you—'

'Always the melodramatic type, weren't you?' A sneer in Smart's voice now. A sense that all was not lost.

'Melodramatic? After what you did?' Anger. 'We trusted you and you—'

'I did what I had to do.'

'Jesus Christ, do you not regret what–?'

'I don't do regrets,' said Smart, glancing sideways and catching a glimpse of the intruder in the wall mirror. Drew confidence from the tears in the eyes. 'Never have, not going to start now, certainly not for the likes of you.'

They were the last words that Dennis Smart ever uttered. He made not a sound as his assailant lunged for him. Did not have time to react, so sudden was the movement. A shove in the back sent him crashing down the stairs. He momentarily appeared to hang in the air, a life in slow motion, a death in freeze-frame, until time resumed and he continued to fall. Smart struck his head three times on the banister and hit the hall floor with a crunching sound, the impact twisting his right leg at a sickening angle.

As his killer walked softly down the stairs, over his broken body and out through the front door, closing it with the quietest of clicks, Dennis Smart lay silent, blood oozing from an ugly head wound, his lifeless eyes staring up at the expensively carved ceiling.

Two weeks later, three men huddled over their pints of bitter, whispering conspiratorially and occasionally glancing up from the table to see if anyone was listening. There was no one to listen, though; it was early on a Sunday evening in the dog days of summer and The Red Lion was deserted apart from a slim young blonde sitting behind the bar, reading the newspaper and ignoring the men in the corner of the snug. This night, last night, tomorrow night, it was always the same, she thought, the same whispered conversations, the same furtive glances, the same ... she gave the slightest of smiles. Tomorrow night would not be the same. Nothing would be the same again at The Red Lion, she thought, returning to her perusal of the paper. Tomorrow night would really give them something to talk about. All she had to do was keep her nerve and the job would be done and she could go home. God, how she wanted to go home. As far away from The Red Lion as possible.

The three of them sat in silence as they played out the final scenes of Dennis Smart's turbulent life amid the gloom of the hospital room, the curtains having been drawn by a nurse to keep out the fading daylight, the door into the ward closed to give them privacy in his final hours. Three of them sitting round the bed, a greying woman in her late fifties, clutching a dry handkerchief on her lap, and a younger couple in their thirties, she blonde, he dark-haired, neither of whom acknowledged each other's

7

presence. No sidled looks, no smiles of reassurance, no squeezed hand in support. There, just not for each other. Then there was Dennis Smart himself, his eyes closed, his breathing laboured, his skin pale. His life almost at an end.

He had not spoken since the accident inflicted such terrible injuries and nothing was said by those watching him dying either, the odd fragments of conversation having long since faded away to be replaced by a heavy and oppressive silence. No one could think of anything to say anyway.

The one who did all the talking at The Red Lion, his voice fast and low, was a wild-haired, wild-eyed man by the name of Baz Garland, a rebel with as many causes as he had been able to get his hands on during his thirty-nine years. His tattered parka bore numerous faded badges, trophies of battles long since fought, reminders of the days when his beloved 'Workers' held sway on the factory floors of the northern industrial city of Hafton. Golden images in his gallery of distorted memories in a world where time had stood still as the city did its best to move on.

A veteran of many a picket line, Baz Garland burned with the fires of injustice. Most people ignored him, realized that those days were long gone and took the view that Garland's anger made him a man best avoided. Some even described him as dangerous, but never to his face. No one wanted to risk the wrath of Baz Garland, no one wanted to spark the fires of his fury. You were never quite sure what he would do; there were rumours among the regulars at the Lion that he had once beaten a man half to death in a row about politics but nobody was quite sure if it was true. And nobody wanted to find out.

There were still some prepared to listen to his rantings, though; not many of them but a few. Next to him in the snug sat a man whose moustache was neatly trimmed and whose close-cropped hair was as suspiciously shiny and black as his leather jacket. Tommy Webb, family man, father-of-three, dole-queue fodder, listened enthralled as Garland gave voice once more to his anger at what had happened to the factory eight months previously. Webb nodded as the words poured out and ignited his dreams of revenge against the people who had closed the plant, throwing 187 men and women out of work. Webb had known the moment that the closure was announced, the notice pinned on the canteen noticeboard by an underling, that it was the end for his ilk; there were no jobs for time-served men his age in 1990s Hafton with its derelict factories and swathes of wire-strewn wasteland.

As Webb listened this night, he was inspired, as every night, by Garland's words and his eyes gleamed as he found himself excited by the reckless way the younger man talked. Baz reminded Tommy of his father, another union firebrand whose fiery oratory had inspired many a wildcat walkout in years gone by. Tommy remembered standing, as a young man, in the crowd outside Smarts one misty November morning, listening to his father's speech before heading out on strike, punching the air as he was carried along in the crowd, not quite sure why he was withdrawing his labour but sure it was the right thing to do.

He remembered the rush of adrenalin, the angry shouts of the men and their bright-eyed excitement at the sense of something happening. In that moment, they, he, would have followed his father anywhere. Listening to Garland, Tommy Webb felt the same pull. It was intoxicating stuff and his fingers tightened round his glass as he thought of his father, sitting frail and twisted in the lounge of the nursing home, his father whose eyes were sunken and dulled, his father whose health had been destroyed by asbestosis caused by years of working on the shop floor at Smarts, his father abandoned by those he trusted to care for him when he was at work. His father waiting for death.

Dennis Smart's family were waiting for death as well. Smart had been brought into Hafton General Hospital a fortnight previously after falling down the stairs when he was alone in the family's large house, which stood on its own in the rural flatlands to the west of the city. The doctors reckoned that he had stumbled and lost his footing; they had hazarded the suggestion that he may have experienced some sort of blackout, having been told by the family that he had been a hard drinker for many years. His wife had told the paramedic that the carpet at the top of the stairs had been loose for months, that she had nagged her husband to do something about it but, as usual, he had waved away her request. She thought he was probably drunk and had tripped over it. Whatever the cause, Dennis Smart had sustained head injuries from which he would never recover.

It had been his wife and daughter-in-law who found him when they came in from a shopping trip. For a few shocked moments, they stared as he lay motionless with blood oozing from a head wound, the crimson tide staining the oak floor that had cost so much to install. Eleanor came to her senses first and called 999 before going outside to watch for the ambulance on the narrow country road.

Left alone in the house with her husband, Margaret sat in silence halfway up the stairs and watched him without displaying emotion. She had thought then that he was dead and now, two weeks later, he nearly was; the doctors had been clear from the outset that the chances of recovery were so slim that it made little sense to hold out any hope. False hope, they'd called it. Don't hold out false hopes, they had said. During the fortnight that followed, there had been nothing to evoke even false hope and Margaret had found herself praying many times that her husband would die and bring it all to an end. She did sometimes wonder if she should feel guilty about entertaining such feelings but concluded that would be hypocrisy.

Margaret had been at home when the final call came from the hospital to say that her husband had taken a dramatic turn for the worse that afternoon. The sister on the phone explained that it would be unwise to wait for evening visiting hours and suggested that the family come in now. It had only been a slight difference in his breathing, she said, but she had seen it all before, knew the signs, knew how rapidly these things could deteriorate in a person so weakened by coma.

Margaret, her son Robert and his wife Eleanor had been in the room at the hospital for a couple of hours now. Waiting. Willing him to die and release them. They could hear the muffled sounds of normal hospital life through the closed door but it seemed like a world away. More than once, Dennis's breathing seemed to stop but each time the family leaned forward, preparing to mark the end, he gave a cough, his chest rose and fell and his eyes flickered, momentarily opening, looking but not seeing. Each time it happened, the family wished that he were gone.

The second man listening to Baz Garland's voice growing ever louder as the drink took hold was Ron Maskell. Good old Ron. Daft Lad Ron, everyone called him, born simple fifty-seven years previously to parents who had him adopted when it became obvious that he would never amount to much. Ron, who smiled even when no one cracked a joke, Ron, who beamed when he saw butterflies in the park, Ron, who still did not understand why he had lost his job sweeping floors at the factory and who had cried when the gates were locked for the last time on that dark afternoon in January and his workmates told him gently that he would never go back.

The girl behind the bar, who was now wiping beer glasses, glanced over as one of the three men laughed loudly. Garland noticed her interest and leaned over the table.

'We sure about her?' he asked the others, in what he assumed to be a whisper. 'I mean, what if she heard what we are doing?'

'Relax,' said Webb, 'she's all right, is Ally.'

'I don't know, mate, you can't be too careful when it comes to—'

'Stop worrying, Baz, man. More interested in getting her hair done, that one, eh, Ron?'

Maskell grinned. 'Oh, aye,' he said. 'You're right there, Tommy.'

'Wouldn't kick her out of bed, mind,' said Webb, perusing her appreciatively. 'She's a nice bit of ass.'

Maskell sniggered but Garland continued to survey her suspiciously for a few moments more until, eventually reassured that she was much more interested in shining glasses than their conversation, he turned back and started speaking again. When Katie Summers was sure that she was no longer being observed, she finished the last of the glasses and resumed her reading of the paper while she waited for the pounding of her heart to fade in her ears. That was the closest she had come to a confrontation with Garland during her time at the pub. She had always viewed him with unease so she willed herself to look unconcerned, as if she had not heard his words or noticed his anxious looks in her direction; it would not do to ruin things so close to the big night, she thought. Too much trust had been invested in her and Blizzard would not want her to make a silly mistake when the job was all but done.

Detective Chief Inspector John Blizzard stepped out of the lift and gave himself a cursory tidy-up, running a hand through his tousled hair before straightening his tie and heading towards Ward 61 of Hafton General Hospital, at the door of which he rang the buzzer. As he waited for someone to answer he contemplated the reason for his presence there; he knew it was wrong, knew only too well that he'd been warned off further intrusion into the Smarts' lives, but he also felt compelled to be there. When no one answered, he rang the buzzer again. This time, the door was opened by a young nurse.

'Visiting time is over, I am afr—' she began.

'DCI Blizzard,' said the inspector, holding up his warrant card and brushing past her. 'Dennis Smart. Where is he?'

'You can't see him,' she said, scuttling after the detective as he strode down the corridor. 'He's not feeling very well and—'

'You can cut the crap, pet, I know he's pegging it.' The inspector gestured to several closed doors. 'Which one is it?'

She hesitated.

'I'll look in them all if I have to,' he said.

'The end one, but—'

'Thank you.'

As Blizzard entered the darkened room, Robert Smart stood up, a furious expression on his face.

'What the hell are you doing here?' he said.

'Heard your dad was on his last legs. Wondered if he'd said anything.'

''You insensitive bastard!' Robert gestured to the man in the bed. 'Do you really think he's in a state to say anything?'

'I guess not. Just thought I'd—'

'Can't you see my husband is dying?' hissed Margaret. 'Why won't you leave us alone? After all my family has suffered.'

'*Your* family has suffered?'

'Get out!' She startled them all with the loudness of her voice as she stood up and pointed to the door. 'You have no right to be here.'

'Maybe so,' said Blizzard. He turned as the sister burst into the room, held up his hands and walked into the corridor. 'OK, OK, I'm going.'

'I'll be complaining to your superior officer about this,' said the sister. 'This is absolutely disgraceful behaviour, a terrible breach of trust, even for you.'

'Arthur Ronald,' said Blizzard over his shoulder, as he walked back down the corridor. 'Detective Superintendent Arthur Ronald at Abbey Road. Extension 216, if my memory serves me right.'

Katie Summers had been working behind the bar at The Red Lion for more than a month and had been intrigued from the beginning by the three men in the snug, even though they were not the reason she was undercover. Western Division CID had drafted in the detective constable from over the water in Lincolnshire because no one would recognize her; John Blizzard and his team were too well known by the local villains to send in one of their own. She had been instructed to gather intelligence on the trade in stolen property said to pass through the back-street pub and the young officer had watched with a growing sense of amazement as televisions, video machines and car radios passed over the bar. 'It's like Dixons,' she had told Colley when checking in one night from the call box near her bedsit. 'I've never seen anything like it, Sarge.' 'I guess it's all sheep rustling where you come from,' the sergeant had replied. 'Or worse....'

She would not miss the Lion when the operation was over but remained disturbed by the three men who conspired every evening in the snug. It was the occasional snatched words that she caught that made her uneasy. *Capitalist scum. Robbing bastards. Ripe for a kicking. Class war.* That and the wild look in Garland's eyes. Summers often wondered if his words were just that. Words. The drink talking. Blizzard seemed certain that was the case, according to Colley, and Summers had heard enough of the DCI's reputation during her time in Hafton not to question his judgement. And yet, she thought as she watched Tommy Webb walk up to the bar, carrying three empty pint glasses, and yet....

'What you reading about, pet?' he asked, as he placed the glasses on the bar.

'The report of Hafton's game against Rotherham.'

'Yeah?' He seemed surprised. 'You follow football, then?'

'Old habits die hard, I guess. My dad always went to the home games. I don't go myself, mind. Just read about it in the paper. Besides, I had a hair appointment yesterday.'

'Thought you might. It looks nice.'

'Thank you. Did you go to the match?'

'Used to but then I lost me job, couldn't afford it after that.' Webb's face clouded over. 'The dole don't pay for no football tickets, Ally. Can I have a whisky chaser with that, pet?'

Summers nodded and reached for the optic.

'Sure thing, boss,' she said.

Blizzard was still smiling as he got into the lift. There'd likely be complaints, he thought, there were always complaints, and there were those who would regard what he had done as an error of judgement, but he had achieved what he set out to achieve. Rattle some cages, let the family know that he had not forgotten what they did. That the death of Dennis Smart would not change anything. That the mealy-mouthed platitudes of the chief constable would not protect them for ever. Besides, the inspector reasoned as he reached for the button, Smart did not deserve a peaceful death. None of them deserved peace, not after what they had done, and no amount of lectures from Arthur Ronald would change the inspector's mind about that.

'Hold the lift, please,' said a voice, and the young nurse he had brushed past in the ward appeared at the door to the lift.

'Hello again.' Blizzard kept his hand pressed on the button and tried to give her a reassuring smile. 'Going down?'

'Would you like me to wait for the next one? I can see I'm not wanted.'

'No need for that.' I must work on that smile, thought Blizzard gloomily, they never came out right. 'Look, I'm glad I've seen you. I owe you an apology. You did not deserve to be spoken to like that back there. Not sure I can hold the door much longer. Are you going down or not?'

She got into the lift.

'Ground floor, please,' she said. 'I'm going to the canteen for my break.'

The door closed and the lift jolted and began to descend. Blizzard looked at the nurse's name badge, struggling as ever to make out the small print. Colley was right, damn him, it was time for a trip to the optician. 'So, do you accept my apology, Nurse … Ruttles? The Ruttles. Weren't they a rock band?'

'It's Rutter,' she said. 'Amanda Rutter. And I've never heard of the Ruttles.'

'They were around in the seventies. Some famous bloke was in them.' The inspector decided that it was time for some Blizzard charm to defuse the situation. Not that it ever worked, that's why he usually left it to Colley, but if there were complaints in the air it was worth a try. 'Can't quite recall his name. Sorry, I'm rambling. Which floor is geriatrics again? It's well past my bedtime. Is that Horlicks I can smell?'

To his surprise, she smiled. A delightful smile, thought Blizzard. Immediately, he remembered Fee back at home. And their unborn child. And felt guilty. Like he always did when he talked to attractive young women these days. Particularly blonde ones.

'No need to apologize,' she said.

'Actually I think there probably is,' said the inspector as the lift continued its downward journey, 'I was out of order back there.'

'Not to the family, I hope.' She lowered her voice even though they were alone. 'I don't like them either, Chief Inspector. Think they're something special, they do. Particularly that Margaret, looks down her nose at everybody. Stuck-up cow. Were you here to arrest them?'

The bluntness of the question caught him by surprise.

'Not sure I should be telling you that,' said the inspector, as the lift reached the ground floor and they stepped out into the corridor. He had detected a slight change in her voice, an edge that was not there before, and he sensed that the time had come for caution. 'If hospitals are anything like police stations, it'd be all over the place by this time tomorrow.'

'Is it something to do with the factory?' she asked, ignoring his comment. 'The one that closed?'

'And why would you say that, Nurse Rutter? You got a reason for asking?' He gave her a hard look. 'Have I, by any chance, been ambushed?'

'OK, I admit it,' she said and glanced along the deserted corridor to make sure they were alone. 'I wanted to talk to you.'

'About?'

'My father was with Smarts. Hasn't worked since they closed it down and my grandfather, he was with them for years and now he's dying.' The words came quickly and the detective let them pour out. 'Have you ever seen someone die of asbestosis, Inspector? It's agonizing. Fighting for every breath. A living death.'

'I know. It's horrible.'

'I very much doubt it.'

'Some of my friends are former railwaymen,' explained the inspector. 'Worked in the sheds. Several of them have died from it.'

'Then you know how terrible it is. And the lawyer says that because Smarts closed and the records have been lost, there's virtually no chance that he'll get any compensation. Or if he does, it'll take that long he'll be dead before it comes through. All we wanted was some money to adapt the house, let him stay with my grandmother. Now he's in a home. My father's very angry about it. Reckons there was something dodgy about what the directors did when they closed the company.'

'Does he know what?'

'Just what he heard in the pub. That they were cooking the books. Look, I know this is unprofessional, Chief Inspector, but I'm glad Dennis Smart is dying.' She looked at him with a confused look on her face. 'Does that make me a bad person?'

'Who knows?' shrugged Blizzard. He tried not to appear interested. 'What's your father's name?'

'Tommy Webb.'

'Never heard of him,' lied Blizzard and started to walk down the corridor. After a few paces, he turned back. 'Eric Idle.'

'What?'

'Eric Idle, he was the one in the Ruttles. Knew it would come to me eventually.' He started walking again. 'Just takes longer these days. Goodnight, Nurse Rutter.'

Dennis Smart stopped breathing. For a minute or so, no one spoke, nor did they look at each other. Margaret grasped her handkerchief a little tighter, Eleanor looked at her feet and Robert walked over to the window, drawing the curtains to stare down onto Hafton city centre as the late-summer sun started to fade and the shadows snaked across the streets. The silence was disturbed by the arrival of the sister a couple of minutes later. She walked over to the bed, leaned down to listen for breathing, then checked for a pulse before shaking her head.

'I'm sorry,' she said, straightening up and glancing at the clock. 'He's gone. Six forty-seven. You will want to spend some time with him, I imagine. Take as long as you wish.'

She walked out into the ward, gently closing the door behind her. Robert turned back from the window and looked down over to the bed as the remaining colour drained from his father's face. He unhooked his coat from the back of one of the chairs.

'Let's get out of here,' he said.

Chapter Two

S*HE WALKED DOWN the corridor and hesitated at the top of the staircase, her heart pounding in her ears, her hand clammy as it gripped the banister. She knew instinctively, knew without even knowing how, that she was not alone in the building. Realized with a sick feeling that this was the moment she had expected, the moment she had dreaded. Not normally a woman prone to fear, she felt cold as she stood at the top of the stairs.*

It was just after 6.45 when John Blizzard returned to Abbey Road Police Station, an ageing collection of portable units standing at the heart of Western Division. Having parked his Granada in the yard, the inspector headed for the first floor CID room, his mood darkening as he walked down the poorly lit corridors. Would the sister have made her complaint yet, he wondered? He guessed that she might have done. She had seemed angry. *Very* angry. They'd bumped heads before but he'd never seen her that annoyed.

On reflection, the inspector had to admit, albeit reluctantly, that barging in on a dying man had not been one of his better ideas. He sighed; he knew that an innate ability to make life difficult for himself was his biggest weakness, always had been. He perked up slightly, however, at the thought that the sister might have reconsidered after a calming cup of tea and decided against complaining. It was a cheering thought and one that the inspector took with him into the CID room, which was empty apart from David Colley. It lasted only until he saw the disbelieving look on the detective sergeant's face as he looked up from his paperwork.

'What on earth were you thinking?' asked the sergeant with a shake of the head.

'Now is that really the way to greet your boss?' Blizzard sat down at one of the desks and tried to look as if the comment had not affected him. 'What happened to respect for your seniors?'

'Not sure they deserve it when they do something this stupid. And I'm not sure you should be that cheerful either. The super's on the warpath. Long time since I've seen him this mad. Slamming doors and everything.'

'I wonder what that's about?'

'Don't play the innocent, guv. You know exactly what it's about. Don't you remember the super saying that the Smarts are off limits?'

'Might have done.' The inspector surveyed his colleague. Despite the hour, Colley was, as ever, smartly turned out, his black hair neatly combed, his round, almost boyish face still clean-shaven and his dark suit crease-free. 'I just hope I can look that good when the little 'un is born. You were up half the night with Laura's teething yet you—'

'Don't change the subject.' Colley glanced at the wall-clock. Even for Blizzard that was remarkable, thought the sergeant; he'd not been in the room for thirty seconds and, crisis or not, he'd already mentioned the blessed baby. 'I'm serious about the super, he's really—'

'Really hacked off, that's what he is!' barked a voice and

a large man appeared at the door. He glared at Blizzard.

'Ah, Arthur,' said Blizzard.

'Don't "Ah, Arthur" me. My office. Now!'

Blizzard sighed as he lowered his feet from the desk and followed the superintendent out of the room. The sergeant shook his head again and jotted twenty-nine seconds down on a piece of paper.

Neither Blizzard nor Ronald spoke as they walked along the corridor towards the superintendent's office. Once inside, Ronald slammed the door and sat down behind his desk. The chair creaked its protest beneath his bulk.

"What on earth were you thinking?' asked the superintendent, as Blizzard drew up a chair. 'I mean, what the hell was going through your mind, man?'

'You're the second person who has asked me that and all I can say is—'

'Do you know who I have just had on the phone? The sister on Ward 61 at the General, that's who. She's bloody livid. Claims you barged in on Smart's deathbed. His *deathbed*, for God's sake!'

'Not sure I would say barged, Arthur, more like—'

'Oh, don't give me any of your crap! Why were you there? After all the trouble we've had with them.'

'Wanted to see if he said anything before he died. Clear his guilty conscience.'

'Guilty conscience, my arse! You know he's been in a coma since they took him in.' Ronald jabbed a finger at him. 'You went out of sheer devilment, John. Sheer bloody devilment. I told you to leave it alone yet you expressly disobeyed my—'

'I can't leave it alone, Arthur. I'm sorry but I really can't. Not after what he did. Not after what they all did. Do you know how many lives were ruined because of—?'

'Oh, don't start that again. We found nothing to suggest wrongdoing and you know that as well as anyone. God help us if the family make a formal complaint.' Ronald looked at his colleague in bewilderment. 'You've let me down, John, you've let me down badly. This is a serious breach of trust and I'm not sure I can protect you if the chief constable comes calling. It was all I could do to save your hide last time.'

'OK, so I overstepped the mark,' said Blizzard, opting for a more conciliatory approach and holding up his hands, 'for which I apologize. I know this puts you in a difficult position, Arthur, but maybe the family won't complain.'

'I would if some insensitive plod came barging in like that, especially if it was only a few weeks since I had sub- mitted a formal complaint about harassment. Yes, I'd put a bloody complaint in, especially at a time of such acute personal grief.'

'Personal grief,' snorted Blizzard. 'That's your problem, you're not thinking it through, none of you is. They weren't pissed off because I intruded on personal grief, they were pissed off because the last thing they want is me raking things up again. There's precious little family love there.'

'Do you really believe that?' said Ronald, giving him a hard look. 'I mean, *really* believe it? Or have you let your- self be blinded by your dislike of the family? Wouldn't be the first time you'd let personal feelings get in the way of an investigation, would it? You've hardly been a paragon of professional police work on this one, have you?'

'I am always professional,' said Blizzard. There was an edge to his voice now. 'You of all people should know that after all these years.'

A heavy silence settled on the room as the friends eyed each other uneasily. They had known each other for years but were very different men. University-educated and married with two teenaged children, Ronald was immaculately dressed, a pudgy, balding man with ruddy cheeks and eyes with bags which sagged darkly. Blizzard was scruffier, broad-chested and wearing his customary dark suit with the tie at half-mast. His hair was tousled as usual.

Before being reunited at Abbey Road, their careers had taken different paths. Following early days together as rookie detectives, Blizzard had remained a CID officer, making his name in the Drugs Squad, while Ronald, ambitious for high rank, had gone into uniform, eventually earning the job he always craved, commanding CID in the constabulary's southern half. One of his first decisions was to demand that Blizzard be promoted to DCI in charge of Western CID, the largest division in Ronald's new patch. The suggestion was opposed by a chief constable wary of Blizzard's maverick tendencies but Ronald persisted until the chief relented. Since then, detection rates had increased in Western and crime had fallen year on year. There were those who believed that Blizzard would be out of a job should it ever be any different.

'Let's change the subject,' said Ronald, noticing his friend's angry expression. 'I see little point in going back over old ground. Colley tells me you want to go into The Red Lion tomorrow night? Do we have enough to make it stick?'

Blizzard nodded, relieved to be discussing something else, something on which both men could agree; the debate surrounding the Smarts inquiry had been a matter of contention between them for months.

'According to young Katie Summers,' said the inspector, 'Monday night is a busy one. Plenty of gear around and virtually all the main players will be there. Fish in a barrel, Arthur, fish in a barrel.'

'Yes, well, you'll hear no argument from me when it comes to the Lion. You going to pull the kid out first?'

'We've told her to call in sick tomorrow. Don't want her anywhere near the place. She's done well, mind, Arthur. Good officer. Colley likes her as well and I trust his judgement.'

'And she is a blonde.' Ronald gave his friend a sly smile, risking humour to ease the tension that still hung in the thick air of the room. 'And you do like blonde detective constables.'

'I shall treat that comment with the disdain it deserves,' said Blizzard but he, too, smiled. Neither of them wanted to fall out. 'I am just saying that young Katie has done a good job.'

'Not thinking of poaching her, are you?' said Ronald suspiciously. 'Not sure Lincs would appreciate that. I had all on to persuade them to loan us to her as it was. They only did it because her gaffer's an old mate of mine.'

'You worry too much. Besides, we *are* one down what with Fee going off on maternity.'

'And whose fault is that?' said Ronald, glancing at the wall-clock and jotting something down on a piece of paper on the desk. 'Three minutes thirty-seven seconds. No chance.'

'What?'

'Colley's sweepstake.' The superintendent held up the paper. 'Quickest mention of the baby, twenty pence a go. One of the girls in the canteen is ahead at the moment, apparently – twenty-three seconds. That's some going.'

Blizzard gave him a rueful look. 'I guess I do bang on about it.'

'And so you should. Man of your age, it's positively miraculous.'

'Thank you for those few kind words,' murmured Blizzard, as he leaned over and picked up the paper. 'Hang on, this says all profits go to Age Concern!'

'No respect any more. Do you want me to have a word with Katie's governor, then?'

'No, I'll talk to her first. See if she wants to come over here.' Blizzard stood up and headed for the door. 'You OK with us going into the Lion tomorrow, then?'

'You know I am, high time the place was closed down. Besides, it might take your mind off the Smarts. I'll ask uniform to sort some bodies.'

'We'll need plenty of them, mind, you know the crackerjacks that get in there,' said the inspector, leaving the office, his voice floating back from the corridor. 'Hey, maybe I can get you a nice telly. Better than the crappy one your missus made you buy.'

'Insufferable,' murmured Ronald as the sound of the inspector's footsteps receded. 'Absolutely insufferable.'

But he was smiling. It was a smile of relief that their argument had not escalated. The sensation did not last long, however, and, face clouding over, he picked up his phone and dialled an internal number.

'You're working late, Pam,' he said into the phone. 'I wonder, is the chief still in?'

'You must be reading each other's minds, sir. He's just asked me to get hold of you. Something about an incident at the hospital? He wants to know if you are free for a meeting first thing tomorrow.'

'I am afraid I am,' sighed Ronald.

Colley had just put the phone down when Blizzard walked

back into the CID room.

'I was worried about you,' said the sergeant. 'You still got your knackers?'

'It's you who should be worrying.' Blizzard flicked a twenty-pence piece onto the desk. 'Did you really think I wouldn't find out?'

'Surprised it took you this long. Been running it for the best part of a week. Call yourself a detective.'

'The only reason I'm not more hacked off is that Arthur has OK'd tomorrow night.'

'Katie will be pleased to hear that. She's heartily sick of The Red Lion and I'm not sure she believes me when I tell her that she's not being followed. She's mentioned it several times in the past few days. Sure I can't tell her?'

'Best not. Don't want her giving the game away. It's nearly over anyway.'

'I guess. Oh, that phone call as you were coming in. Some nurse from the General. Said she should not really be ringing you but said you'd like to know that Dennis Smart is dead. Didn't sound like your normal contact there.'

'It'd be Alison Rutter. Just met her. Her dad worked at Smarts.' The inspector walked out into the corridor. 'Wherever you go in this city, you find fallout from the closure of that factory.'

'Blonde?'

Blizzard walked back into the room and stared at his sergeant. 'What?'

'This Alison Rutter. Was she blonde?'

'Goodnight, David,' repeated Blizzard and walked out into the corridor again.

'Night, guv,' grinned Colley. His mobile rang and he fished it out of his jacket pocket. 'Hi, love. How is she? ...

Yeah? Maybe we can get some sleep tonight, then. Do you want me to pop into a chemist and get some more on my way home? ... No, won't be long, just got a couple of things to sort.'

He replaced the phone in his pocket and ran a hand over tired eyes.

The red-brick factory building stood dark and silent at the end of King Street as night settled on the city. The street had once been a bustling city-centre thoroughfare; even ten years previously, there had been numerous businesses trading here, each one a clanking and clattering centre of activity, shifts clocking on, shifts clocking off, men in overalls heading for smoky street-corner pubs full of bustle and chatter, The Red Lion among them. One by one, though, the factories had closed their gates, victims of 1980s' recession, eventually leaving King Street alone and neglected.

Smart and Co. was the last of the firms to go. An engineering company, it could trace its beginnings back to the Victorian industrialist Jebediah Smart. Old Man Jebediah – everyone in the city knew him as Old Man Jebediah – was a white-bearded patrician whose factory employed 240 men at its height. Fathers and sons lived out their lives hunched over the firm's machines and families relied on its pay packets; people lived and died but the factory kept on working, with Old Man Jebediah's stern image staring down from the boardroom wall. However, not even Smarts could last for ever and, in time, its story became like all the others as contracts dried up when the city's shipyards closed, the railway works ran out of work and the bridge-builders fell silent.

The decision to close had come at a brief board meeting on an icy mid-January morning, after which the directors had a junior clerk pin the notice on the canteen wall and issued a terse press release announcing that the business was no longer viable, blaming dwindling order books. That was *their* story, the workers said; many saw things differently and there were dark mutterings, accusations, insinuations, angry exchanges with management over accounts more remarkable for what they did not say rather than what they did. It was all for nought because Smarts locked its gates within thirty-six hours. No consultation with the unions, no rescue plans, no meetings to thank the workers, just a padlock on the gates and tears from Daft Lad Ron Maskell. The hurt still ran deep.

The factory had stood empty and dark for eight months now and, shortly before midnight, a figure carrying a petrol can approached the gates, glanced along the deserted street and slipped through a gap in the fence. Ten minutes later, an orange glow appeared in one of the building's side windows.

With the last of the drinkers dispatched into the night, Katie Summers left The Red Lion, stepping out into the deserted street and beginning the short walk to the run-down bedsit where she had lived since the undercover operation began. Colley had acknowledged from the beginning that it was an unpleasant place to live but said that it made for a perfect cover should anyone suspect her. It was only a short distance from the pub and she always walked when her shift finished, confident that the self-defence techniques she had learned as a police officer would be enough to defend her against any drunk who tried it on.

As she turned the corner onto the main road, something made her look back and she saw a figure at the other end of the street, heading slowly in her direction. Summers tensed and stood watching him for a few moments until he lurched off the pavement, staggered slightly and headed down a side street. Hearing him retching, she gave a loud sigh of relief and turned for home. As she did so, a fire engine, lights flashing, sped past her in the direction of the Smarts factory.

Chapter Three

STANDING AND LOOKING *down at the hallway, she tried to retain her composure. She peered in vain for movement in the half-light, strained to hear any sound which would identify the location of the intruder. Something that would give her the edge. Nothing stirred and she stood for the best part of a minute listening to the silence of the building. When it came, though, the noise was behind her.*

'Your governor not here?' asked the fire investigator as David Colley walked across the empty car-park in front of the Smarts factory. 'He's usually banging on about this place, isn't he?'

'He's taken the morning off.' The sergeant perused the front of the building, its harsh red-brick lines softened by the early-morning mist. 'No damage then?'

'Fairly minor. Just like last week.' The fire officer led the way as they pushed their way through the creaking glass front door and entered the gloom of the small reception area. 'Hey, I just heard, is it true that Blizzard's going to be a dad?'

'Don't you bloody start. I have enough with him banging on about the blessed sprog. Not even Jesus had a build-up like this. Going to give a whole new meaning to Christmas.'

'Like that, is it?' grinned the fire officer.

They pushed their way through a set of swing doors and stood for a few moments as they allowed their eyes to grow accustomed to the grey light that filtered through the high windows onto the dusty shop floor. Listen hard enough, thought Colley in the heavy silence, and you could still hear the clatter of machines, the voices of the men, the.... He shook his head irritably; getting too like Blizzard, he thought. Let the place speak to you, the inspector always said, let it tell you what it wants to tell you. Him and his bloody sayings, thought the sergeant, and gave a slight smile. Even when he was not with him the curmudgeonly old bastard was still there.

'My mate worked here, you know,' said the fire officer, breaking into the sergeant's reverie.

Colley sighed as he heard Blizzard's voice again, reminding him that you did not have to go far in the Division to encounter someone with a link to Smarts, a reason to resent those who had allowed it to happen. It had been the inspector's constant mantra ever since the factory closed, his justification for refusing to give up on the inquiry, dead as it appeared to be.

'Twenty-eight years,' continued the firefighter, 'then the bastards closed it down without a by-your-leave. Just came in one morning and that was it. Criminal, it was. Your boss is right, you know, there was something off about it.'

'Except we found nothing to support that,' said the sergeant, rehearsing old arguments as the fire officer led the way across the floor, their shoes crunching on broken glass. 'Just a lot of pub talk. If I arrested everyone mentioned in pub talk, there'd be no one left on the outside.'

'Maybe so, but there's plenty of folks round here reckoned they were on the take. I heard that they had a secret stash that the taxman knew nowt about. In the Cayman Islands, my mate always reckons.'

'Cayman Islands,' snorted the sergeant. 'Like I said, our Fraud Squad couldn't find anything to back any of it up. Smarts just went under, end of. Wouldn't be the first time a firm has gone bust, won't be the last, especially in this city. There's nothing more to it than that.'

'There's plenty would disagree.'

'I'm sure they would,' said the sergeant as they walked into a dingy narrow corridor to be assailed by the rank aroma of smoke, sharp at the back of their throats. 'Not that it matters to Dennis Smart.'

'Yeah, someone said he'd taken a header down the stairs.'

'You didn't get it from me, Les, but he died last night.'

'Explains why the son was in such a foul mood when he turned up here.' The fire officer noticed the detective's questioning look. 'He's the keyholder. We called him out.'

The fire officer pushed open a door to reveal a small storeroom where the smell of smoke was particularly strong.

'This is it,' he said. 'Where it started.'

'You sure it's arson?'

'What else could it be?' The fire officer nodded at a pile of charred papers on the floor. 'Old brochures or something. Fairly half-hearted attempt, if you ask me. Probably burned for a few minutes then petered out. Would probably have died down on its own if we had not been called. Gob on it and it'd have gone out.'

Colley crouched down and peered at the papers.

'Not sure it was a serious effort to burn the place down,' continued the fire officer. 'Kids, like as not.'

'I guess so,' said Colley, as the two men walked back

down the corridor and crossed the shop floor again. 'That's twice in two weeks now, mind. Thought they'd stopped doing it.'

'Nah, we're always getting called to places like this. Derelict buildings attract them like flies. Little toerags. See?' The fire officer gestured up to the succession of shattered windows lining the room. 'They've put out every single one of them since the place closed. Not that it matters, though: I heard they were going to flatten the place and build flats.'

'Apparently.' They emerged into the grey of the morning and Colley looked along the street at the row of derelict and vandalized factories. 'Though not quite sure who'd want to live here.'

'There was a time,' said the firefighter sadly. 'There was a time.'

'This is all we need,' said Robert Smart as he stood at the living-room window and stared out across Larch House's perfectly manicured lawns at the elderly gardener clipping the hedges. Robert turned to the two women, who were sitting on the sofa drinking tea. 'I mean, isn't it? The last thing we need?'

'I imagine your father would agree,' murmured Margaret.

'You know what I mean. His death will have the police back, no doubt.' Robert returned his gaze to the garden. 'Snooping about. Asking questions. Blizzard and that bloody sergeant of his. God, I hate them. If I had my way....'

'Oh, do calm down, dear,' said his mother. 'This isn't helping anyone.'

'Why should they come back anyway?' asked Eleanor,

reaching for her tea. 'It's an accidental death, isn't it? The police don't take much notice of them. I know that from when I worked for them in London. They can't wait to get them signed off.'

'Not sure that applies to Blizzard,' grunted Robert.

'Even if it didn't,' said his mother, 'I think it highly unlikely that he would dare do anything after his little outburst last night, do you? The sister was ringing his boss as we were leaving and Blizzard knows that I only have to pick up the phone to his chief constable.'

'Maybe.'

'Maybe yes, Robert. When I talked to the chief constable a few weeks ago, he promised me that the inquiry was at an end. I hardly think he's going to change his mind once he hears what Blizzard did last night, do you? From what I hear, he has little time for the man.'

'Yes, but you know Blizzard. He's unlikely to—'

'Forget him,' said his mother. 'We should be much more concerned about the arson last night. That's two in a fortnight. I thought you said it had stopped.'

'So did I,' said Robert thoughtfully as he sat down in one of the armchairs. He noticed his mother's concerned expression. 'Don't worry about it, it's probably just kids mucking about. Besides, why do we care if the place burns down? Save us having to demolish it. Might even stop the planners dragging their feet.'

'Assuming it is kids.' His mother frowned. 'What if it's another warning, though?'

Robert reached for his tea. It was cold.

'I said I'd sort it,' he said.

Chapter Four

S HE TENSED AS *she heard someone walking slowly down the corridor towards her. Then the breathing. Close. Heavy. Familiar from her nightmares. Afraid to confront her killer, she continued to stare down into the hallway as if fascinated by something on the floor.*

'Don't turn round,' said a voice she knew well.

'Why?' She tried to sound calm although her trembling voice betrayed her. 'You scared to face me?'

'Always the melodramatic type, weren't you, pet?' A sneer in the voice.

'Melodramatic? After what you did?' Anger. 'I trusted you and you....'

Her voice tailed off and she glanced sideways and caught a glimpse of the intruder in the wall mirror.

'You don't need to take the morning off, John, really you don't,' said Fee Ellis, sitting down on the sofa and taking a sip of her coffee. She tried not to let her exasperation show. 'You don't need to fuss round like a mother hen. I'll be fine.'

'I'm working tonight, the Red Lion job, said I'd go in late,' said the inspector, taking a seat next to her and patting her hand reassuringly. 'What with the baby due in a couple of weeks, you need all the help and support you can get.'

'What happened to the John Blizzard who worked all the hours God gave?'

'He met you.' He leaned over to peck her on the cheek. 'And she changed him.'

'That's right,' she said darkly. 'Blame me.'

It was shortly after nine in the morning and they were sitting in the living room of the inspector's detached house in one of the villages to the west of Hafton. After discovering that she was pregnant, the young detective constable had spent more time at the house and was now living there virtually full-time. Neither of them had made a conscious decision to move in together but it seemed to have happened and Blizzard, a loner before he took up with her, had found himself constantly surprised by his growing domestic instincts.

'Anything you need?' he asked for the fifth time that morning. He glanced at the mug in her hand. 'Another coffee?'

'You've just made this one.'

'Anything else you need, then?' Normally highly adept at picking up nuances, he continued to miss them this time. Had done so for weeks. He stood up. 'Biscuit, maybe. I'll get you a nice bisc—'

'What I need is for you to sod off back to work instead of hanging around here making the place look untidy!'

'Yes, but....' Wounded by the sharpness of her tone and silenced by a look, the inspector looked at her unhappily and sat down again.

'Look, I know you think you're being helpful,' she said, her voice softer now, 'and I appreciate it, I really do, but it really would be much better if you were back at Abbey

Road chewing the head of some poor underling.'

The inspector's mobile rang. Fee looked at the phone lying on the side table.

'There's one now,' she said. The phone kept ringing. 'You not going to answer it? Might be important.'

'Not as important as you.'

'You know I may have to kill you, don't you?'

He stared at her uncertainly.

'Answer the bloody phone!' she said.

The inspector gave a sigh and reached out and put the phone to his ear.

'Blizzard.'

'You coming in this morning?'

'Not sure.' Blizzard glanced at Fee. 'Colley,' he mouthed. 'I may stay here for a couple more—'

'No, he won't!' she shouted. 'Just get him out of my hair, Dave! Straightening things all the time! Puffing up bloody cushions, for God's sake! And I can't move for bleeding cups of coffee! I wouldn't care but they all taste like shit!'

Colley gave a low laugh at the other end of the phone.

'Yes, thanks for your support, Sergeant,' said Blizzard. The inspector waited until Fee had walked into the kitchen, where he heard her pouring her coffee down the sink. 'I just don't understand her, David, I really don't. One moment she's OK and the next....'

'One thing I learned when Jay was about to pop our little 'un was never argue with a heavily pregnant woman. I'd have rather faced down some scumbag off his face on smack. They tend to be more rational.'

'I guess,' sighed Blizzard. 'What's so important that I have to come in, then?'

'There was another fire at Smarts last night, looks iffy. And on a similar theme the Angel of Death wants to see us. Something about Dennis Smart. Reynolds was being very mysterious about it, you know what he's like when he's found something. Said you'd want to be there. He sounded quite pleased with himself.'

'Twenty minutes.' Blizzard put his phone in his pocket and walked into the kitchen where Fee was washing her mug. 'Well, if you're sure.'

'I'm sure.'

'I'll go, then.' The inspector gave her another kiss. 'Duty and all that.'

'You just be careful,' she said affectionately, this time returning the kiss.

'Aren't I always?'

She patted her swollen stomach. 'Always?' she said.

Blizzard looked confused.

'You worry too much,' said Fee. She waited for him to leave the house, listening for the slam of the front door. 'You know, I quite fancy a cup of coffee and a nice biscuit.'

Robert Smart glanced round to make sure that he was not being followed as he turned into the side street on the fringes of the city centre. The last thing he wanted was for someone to see him going into the accountants' the morning after his father's death. It would not present the right image at what was supposed to be a time of mourning, he reasoned. Risky or not, the trip had been necessary, though. Robert was not about to let a silly mistake ruin everything. Not now. Not after they'd been so careful.

Six doors down the street, he stopped at a neat white double shop-front, outside of which was parked a gleaming new Mercedes. Robert glanced at the car and peered through the frosted window of the building, just able to make out of the figure of a woman behind a desk. Robert stepped into the neatly furnished office to be greeted by a bright smile from the receptionist.

'Good morning, Mr Smart,' she said.

'Good morning, Emma, is he in?'

She nodded and Smart walked through into the office.

'Ah, Robert,' said a thin young man in a sharp black suit, coming out from behind the desk, shaking his visitor's hand and gesturing for him to draw up a chair. 'How nice to see you.'

It did not sound to Robert that Henry Gallen meant it.

'Tea?' asked Gallen.

'Please,' said Robert.

Gallen walked back into the reception area. As Robert sat and listened to him instructing Emma to make the drinks, he looked round the office with its tidy furnishings, its gleaming filing cabinets, its well-watered pot plants and the walls lined with expensive paintings. Robert gave a slight smile; such a contrast from the murky world into which the Smarts had dragged Henry Gallen and a symbol of the fact that Robert had him exactly where he wanted him. Not that Gallen had complained at first. The money had been good, very good, and the accountant had only started to protest when he fully realized the enormity of what he was being asked to do.

The relationship had begun some years previously when the Smarts' directors came up with the idea of skimming off the profits from their engineering firm. It was Jason Heavens' idea initially; he could see hard times ahead, clients closing down, increasing competition from abroad, and urged the others to cream off what they could before the firm faltered. Pocket the profits, cook the books, hide true earnings from the taxman, argued Heavens. It was the only way to go. Not that he needed to do much

41

convincing; the others conveniently ignored any misgivings they might have had when they saw the kind of figures that Heavens was talking about.

It was also Heavens who advised that a big account-ancy firm would be less likely to collude in the subterfuge required to make their plan work. Too much potential for things to go wrong, he said, suggesting instead that they use a small outfit, one that would, in his words, be more grateful.

Robert, not a director of the company but operating as its fixer, set out to find someone who had just started out in business, one hungry for success, hungry full stop, one who may be prepared to turn a blind eye to transac-tions of a dubious nature if the rewards were good enough. Henry Gallen, then only 25, was one such man and in the years that the Smarts had been his client, his company had quadrupled its profits and Gallen had enjoyed the trappings of his growing fortune. Henry Gallen owed the Smarts and both he and Robert knew it.

'How's your father?' asked Gallen, returning with a tray bearing two cups of tea. He placed it on the desk and sat down. 'Still the same?'

'That's why I'm here. He died last night.'

'I am so sorry, Robert. He was a fine—'

'Oh, cut the slaver, Henry. We both know he was a Grade A bastard.' Robert Smart leaned forward. 'But his death does leave us with a problem, does it not? I want you to help us solve it. I've got a little job for you.'

'What sort of little job?' asked Gallen suspiciously.

'One of a fiscal nature.'

'I told you last time, I've done with all that. I appreciate what—'

'You're in too deep for that kind of talk.' Robert gestured

round the office. 'Like it or not, all this is built on our cash.'

'I could refuse to do any more.'

Robert did not respond immediately but poured the tea and handed a cup and saucer to the accountant. He noticed that Gallen had started to sweat as he waited for a response.

'You could,' said Robert at length, sitting down and slowly stirring sugar into his drink, 'but it would not be a particularly wise move, would it now? I thought I made that clear last time, Henry. Just as we have shown ourselves grateful for all your assistance, so we are equally capable of showing our ... how shall we phrase it? ... displeasure. You, of all people, should know what we are capable of. If you've forgotten, maybe have a word with Edward Fothergill.'

Silence settled on the room as Gallen stared unhappily at his client.

'What's the job?' he asked eventually, a tone of resignation in his voice.

'Just before my father died, we received a visit from our old friend Blizzard. In the hospital.'

'I thought you said that he had been taken care of,' said Gallen quickly. 'You said the investigation had been closed down.'

'I thought it had been but, clearly, our chief inspector is not in the mood to let things go. It'll probably amount to nothing but I don't want to take any risks so I want to move our money.'

'Why, Robert? The police didn't work it out last time, why should this be any different? I was very careful and they're in the Stone Age when it comes to this kind of thing.'

'I'm sure they are but I can't risk it. I want the money

belonging to my parents moved and I want it moving today.'

'And Rawcliffe and Heavens? Do I move their cash?'

'I'll talk to them and let you know.' Smart drained his cup and stood up. 'Don't let me down, Henry.'

Once he had left the building, Henry Gallen sat staring at the wall for a long time.

Having experienced a night disturbed by dreams of The Red Lion, Katie Summers took a quick shower in the communal bathroom then, wrapped in a towel, walked back along the landing to her bedsit, where she started to pack a small suitcase. She looked round the little room with its dingy wallpaper and threadbare carpet and gave a shake of the head. She would not miss it. In no way would she miss it. Summers clicked her bag closed, glanced at her watch – she was very early – and walked over to look down onto the street. Something made her glance to her right where she noticed, partly concealed behind the parked cars, a man leaning against a lamp post, his face hidden under an anorak hood. Just for a moment, he looked up but she did not recognize him. As he moved off down the street, she shook her head again.

'Dave's right,' she murmured, 'this job does turn you paranoid.'

She sat down on the sofa, picked up a magazine and began to wait.

By 10.30, Blizzard and Colley were in the post-mortem room at the General Hospital, watching Peter Reynolds busy himself round the body of Dennis Smart. Colley assumed his customary position leaning against the wall and Blizzard stood near the table, looking down at the corpse. Colley smiled; if the inspector had disliked Smart then he disliked Peter Reynolds even more. Encounters between the DCI and the Home Office pathologist had long since assumed legendary status at Abbey Road. Colley was always bombarded by requests from colleagues for detailed reports when he got back to the station after such tetchy encounters. Every word, every aside, every look assumed a cachet when it came to meetings between Blizzard and Reynolds and Dave Colley knew how to exploit it.

For his part, Blizzard eyed Reynolds with his customary lack of enthusiasm. The pathologist, a balding, middle-aged little man with piggy eyes gleaming out of a chubby face, and dressed as ever in a shabby, ill-fitting black suit, gave the impression that he liked being around death. As often, he was humming as he worked. Neither detective could make out the tune.

'You're going to love me, Blizzard,' said the pathologist, ceasing his humming but not looking up.

'Why, you emigrating?'

Colley resolved to remember the quip.

'I shall ignore that comment,' said Reynolds.

'Please don't.' Blizzard glanced at his watch. 'Look, are we going to be here long? Only I have something else important to attend to.'

'Diapers to buy, I imagine,' said Reynolds, smiling as he glanced up and saw the inspector glaring at him. 'God knows what the delightful Ms Ellis sees in you. Pretty young thing like her.'

Before Blizzard could reply, the pathologist looked back at the body.

'Tell me, Inspector,' he said, 'how do you think our friend died?'

'I thought you were paid your hugely inflated salary to

tell me those kind of things.'

Colley wondered if it was inappropriate to jot the comments down in his pocketbook; this promised to be one of the better encounters and he was desperate to remember every word. He could visualize the scene in the canteen now.

'Just humour me,' said Reynolds, straightening up. 'What would you surmise to be the cause of his death?'

'Lost his footing, apparently. The doctors seem to think he might have had some sort of blackout, probably after a few too many, but the wife reckons there's a loose bit of carpet. Kept badgering him about it. Anyways, no one has told us anything to suggest anything other than it being an accident.' Blizzard turned to his sergeant. 'Have they?'

'Everything points to him slipping and taking a header down the stairs,' nodded Colley.

'Perhaps not,' said the pathologist.

'You reckon it's dodgy, Doc?'

Reynolds gave Colley a long, hard look.

'As you well know, Sergeant,' he said, 'I do not appreciate being called Doc. I expect such lack of respect from your colleague here but I had rather hoped you were above that kind of thing. And, yes, I am disinclined to believe that he died as the result of an accidental fall. I tend to think that your man was murdered.'

'Murdered?' exclaimed Blizzard. 'None of the doctors mentioned anything about an assault. I only pressed for a PM to piss the family off.'

'Setting aside your questionable methods, Inspector, I have always regarded the study of the dead as a much more exact science than that of the living.' Reynolds looked at the body. To the detectives, it seemed an almost affectionate look. 'However, in defence of my colleagues, his

X-ray did indeed show injuries consistent with what your sergeant so delightfully refers to as a header down the stairs.'

'In which case,' said Blizzard, 'surely it is reasonable to assume—?'

'I find that assumption is a dangerous thing.' Reynolds looked slyly at the inspector. 'You've been in the job long enough to know not to take anything at face value, surely?'

Colley grinned, wiping the look from his face when he saw Blizzard glance in his direction.

'Personally,' continued Reynolds, 'I think that Dennis Smart was pushed.'

'Pushed?' exclaimed Blizzard. 'What on earth makes you think that he was pushed?'

'See that?' Reynolds turned the body over and pointed to the incision he had made in the back. 'That has revealed a fracture of the vertebrae. Only small, I grant you, and one that only the truly skilled eye would notice, but a fracture all the same. The X-ray has confirmed it.'

'So? He probably did it when he hit the floor.'

'The ill-informed person might indeed think so, Inspector.' Reynolds walked over to the sink and began to wash his hands. 'But, for all it would not in itself cause his death, it is consistent with an injury I saw some years ago.'

'And that was a murder, was it?'

'There would be little point in me recounting the tale if the victim died of natural causes, would there now?' Reynolds turned round from the sink while drying his hands with a towel. 'As I recall, a long-suffering woman pushed her partner down the stairs. I'm surprised that the delightful Fee has not tried pushing you down the stairs. I understand you keep boring the arse off everyone else about the impending arrival.'

Blizzard pursed his lips. 'Are you sure about this?'

'What, that you're boring the arse off—?'

'I mean the blasted injury!' snapped Blizzard. 'You're the only one putting forward this hare-brained theory.'

'Hare-brained it may be, Inspector, but I'm prepared to stand up in court and repeat it.' Reynolds gave another sly smile as he walked back to the table. 'It's why they pay me the hugely inflated salary. Mind, I'm not really surprised that no one else picked it up. Why would they? The doctors had been told it was an accident, he clearly had severe head injuries, and he was as good as dead from the moment he hit the floor anyway, so why look for evidence to the contrary?'

'Yes, but—'

'Why do you keep doubting my word, Inspector? Everyone knows you have been itching to reopen the inquiry into Smarts. Like I said, you should be grateful.' As Blizzard stalked out of the room without replying, the pathologist murmured, 'No, don't thank me.'

Outside in the corridor, Blizzard glowered at the sergeant.

'One day,' he said, 'I'll kill him. I really will.'

'Please don't,' said Colley as they started walking, 'I haven't bought a cup of tea for years.'

Chapter Five

SHE MADE NOT a sound as her assailant lunged at her. Did not have time to react, so sudden was the movement. A shove in the back sent her crashing down the stairs. She momentarily appeared to hang in the air, a life in slow motion, a death in freeze-frame, until time resumed and she continued to fall. She struck her head three times on the banister and hit the hall floor with a crunching sound, the impact twisting her leg at a sickening angle. As her killer walked softly down the stairs, stepping over her broken body and out through the front door, closing it with the quietest of clicks, she lay silent, blood oozing from an ugly head wound, her lifeless eyes staring up at the ceiling.

'Murdered?' exclaimed Arthur Ronald, aghast.

'Murdered,' beamed Blizzard as they sat in the super-intendent's office later that morning. The inspector's mood had significantly improved since leaving the hospital. 'Who'd have thought it, eh? Reynolds reckons he was pushed down the stairs and, last time I checked, that's against the law of the land. Almost worth an investigation, wouldn't you say?'

'How come Reynolds was doing a PM anyway? No one mentioned even a suspicion that this was anything other than an accident.' The superintendent narrowed his eyes. 'This has better not be you pulling a fast one, John.'

'Who, me?' Blizzard tried to look innocent.

'Don't try it on. I can always tell when you're hiding something.'

Another facial expression he would have to work on, thought Blizzard. Not that he cared really; despite his dislike of Reynolds, the inspector had felt a lightening of the heart from the moment he heard that Dennis Smart's death was murder. The collapse of Smarts was unfinished business and John Blizzard did not like unfinished business.

'All I said to the hospital,' explained Blizzard, noticing that his boss had continued to look at him suspiciously, 'was that given the nature of the accident, and the background to the case, a PM might be wise. They weren't particularly happy about it.'

'So you were fishing?'

'Maybe so, but look what I caught.'

'This is the last thing we need, it really is,' sighed Ronald. He shot Blizzard a sour look. 'Are you listening to me? The last thing.'

'Don't blame me, Arthur, I'm not the one who pushed him down the stairs. Anyway, last thing or not, even the chief must see the sense in reopening the inquiry now.'

'God knows what he'll say. I've just come from a bollocking on your behalf after your little performance at the hospital last night. You're bloody lucky the family hasn't made a formal complaint. And there's no reason to look so cheerful. This will open a whole nest of vipers, this will.'

'Very vivid metaphor, Arthur. Well done.'

'God, I hate you when you're in a good mood. I take it you want to go to see the Smarts?'

'Has to be done, Arthur. Professional approach and all that. I'm sure you understand.'

Ronald nodded. He understood only too well.

'OK, OK, point taken. Maybe you *were* right. Maybe there *was* something more to the closure of Smarts, but it doesn't mean I want you to close your mind to other possibilities,' said Ronald, raising his voice as the inspector headed out of the office. 'And behave yourself when you're there!'

'Like I would ever do anything else,' said Blizzard from the corridor, 'After all, as I think we have just proved, I'm pretty much infallible.'

'Insufferable, more like,' murmured Ronald as the sound of the inspector's footsteps receded down the corridor. 'Absolutely bloody insufferable.'

This time, he was not smiling. The superintendent had not navigated the turbulent waters of the police service for so long without knowing trouble when he saw it.

Just after noon, Katie Summers left the bedsit without glancing back at the dismal room in which she had lived for more than a month. As someone from a country force, the young detective had found working in the city challenging and the room had come to symbolize everything she disliked about Hafton. She would not be sad to head back to the relative quiet of Lincolnshire's rural beat with its expanses of farmland and its slower pace of life. Nevertheless, she thought, as she slammed the door behind her and clattered down the uncarpeted stairs, she had to admit, albeit reluctantly, that she had enjoyed parts of the experience. The thrill of surveillance, the frisson of fear when people looked at her the wrong way, the rush of adrenalin when she had to talk quickly to allay suspicions.

She had loved ringing Colley at home each night after her shift finished. The sergeant's voice had come to mean so much to her as the days had turned into weeks, his measured tones providing the reassurance that she had so badly needed during her time undercover. Sometimes, he would be cradling his one-year-old daughter if it was one of those nights when Laura could not sleep. Recalling those occasions as she reached the bottom of the stairs, Summers smiled at memories of the sergeant dividing his conversation between them; his two ladies of the night, he had called them. Summers would miss their late-night chats. Colley had been the one thing that had kept her sane.

Summers had also, she thought, as she opened the front door for the last time, enjoyed knowing that John Blizzard appreciated what she was doing. Even though she was from another force, she had heard enough about Blizzard to know that not many people received much encouragement from the DCI. Summers had only met him once, had only met Colley once, for that matter, when the Hafton officers travelled south to brief her at her local police station in Lincolnshire, away from the prying eyes of Hafton villainy. Now, with the job done, she would meet them again. She looked forward to that.

Walking into the street, she saw that the man was back, this time standing in front of the newsagent's, pretending to read the paper but really watching her. Or so she thought. As with the other occasions on which she had seen him, Summers could not be sure. Increasingly, she had difficulty differentiating between fact and fiction. The thrill of adventure had morphed into something else. Something darker. Something more confusing. As Colley had often said during those late night chats, working undercover turned your mind and she'd been at it for weeks, keeping up the act, watching every word, making sure she was not being followed when she left work. No wonder she was jumpy, she thought as she stopped herself staring at the man. It would not do to make a mistake at this late hour of the operation. She was glad it was at an end.

'Time to get out,' she murmured, walking briskly along the street. After a couple of hundred metres, she gave a quick glance back but the man had not moved. 'Definitely time to get out.'

At the far end of the terrace, a battered Ford Escort pulled into a gap between parked cars and the passenger-side door swung open to reveal a young man, features concealed beneath a baseball cap. Katie Summers felt her heart stall.

'Hiya, Ally, gel, haven't seen you for ages. Need a lift?' shouted the man loud enough for anyone walking past to hear. He lowered his voice so that only she could hear. 'Nick Towler, Western CID. Might be worth giving me a quick peck on the cheek when you get in. Make it look like we know each other.'

Summers clambered into the vehicle and did as she was told. As the car pulled away, she looked through the rear window towards the shop but now the man had gone.

'Boy, am I glad to see you,' she said. 'Thought I saw someone watching me.'

'Don't worry about it.'

'That's what Sergeant Colley said but I'm not so sure that—'

'Believe me, don't worry about it,' repeated Towler. He noticed her uncertain look and gave her a nod of reassurance. 'Honest, don't worry.'

'Maybe you're right. The sarge says all undercover officers go loopy in the end.'

'That they do,' grinned Towler, slowing the vehicle as it
approached a crossroads. 'We do need to be careful, mind,
so lie as low as you can as we approach Abbey Road, yeah?
The last thing we want is one of our scroats seeing you
going into the cop shop. Be about ten minutes.'

As she shrank back into the seat, she felt a sudden rush
of emotion and started to cry.

'You OK?' asked Towler, glancing across at her.

'Sorry,' she said, rubbing the tears from her eyes.
'Pathetic, really.'

'You have a good blub. From what I hear, you've
deserved it.'

As the vehicle passed the end of Haverton Street and
her tears subsided, Summers sat up a little and allowed
herself a surreptitious look at the Lion before shrinking
back again when a couple of men emerged from the pub's
doorway. She recognized them as regulars. A few moments
later, as the car passed King Street, she tried the exercise
again, this time looking down towards the old Smarts
factory. A lone figure was standing outside the gates,
staring at the building. She only caught the briefest of
glances, and the face was concealed beneath a parka hood
but she wondered if it was Baz Garland.

Chapter Six

'MURDERED?' EXCLAIMED MARGARET SMART. 'You're saying my husband was murdered?'

'I am,' said Blizzard. He and Colley were standing in the middle of the large living room of Larch House; a female uniformed constable was by the door. 'The pathologist says that someone pushed him down the stairs.'

'What kind of bloody trick is this, Blizzard?' exclaimed Robert, who was sitting next to Eleanor on the sofa. 'The hospital said the post-mortem was a matter of routine and now here you are concocting some cock-and-bull story.'

'The pathologist would beg to differ about—'

'My father's death was accidental and that's all there is to it,' said Robert flatly. 'The doctors agreed. *You* agreed, for God's sake, Blizzard. Nobody mentioned anything about anyone pushing him down the stairs.'

'Is there any chance that the pathologist could be wrong?' asked Margaret.

'Believe me, I would like nothing more.' Blizzard tried to look vaguely sympathetic. 'Look, I know this is difficult for you all to come to—'

'Oh, cut the bullshit!' said Robert. 'This is exactly what you wanted, you bastard! You're loving every minute of this.'

'I would never wish anyone to come to a—'

'Cobblers!' Robert walked over to stare out of the window. 'You hated my father. You hate all of us. As far as I'm concerned, you're just a parasite who—'

'Robert,' said his mother sharply.

Her son gave her a look but did not argue, instead staring moodily out over the lawns.

'He is right, though, Inspector,' said Margaret, turning to the detective. 'You have done little to disguise your belief that we are somehow guilty of a misdemeanour. I imagine you will regard Dennis's death as a reason to start digging around into the circumstances surrounding the closure of the factory again?'

'The background may reveal some salient information, yes.'

'Salient information!' snorted Robert. 'You just can't leave it alone, can you?'

'It was not me who pushed him.'

'And you think one of us did?' said Margaret. Her voice had an edge now. 'Is that what you think, Inspector? That one of us murdered him?'

They all looked at him expectantly.

'It's far too early to draw any conclusions,' said Blizzard, choosing his words carefully. 'However, we will need to take statements from you all.'

'But we were out when he had his fall!' exclaimed Eleanor. 'We all were. We were shopping in Hafton, me and Margaret, then we had lunch at Charlie's in the market square. We've got the receipts to prove it.'

'Then you have nothing to fear.' Blizzard glanced over to the window. 'Can you prove where you were, Robert?'

'I was at the planning department at City Hall. Talking about what to do with the factory site once the place has been pulled down.'

'Anyone verify you were there?'

'A chap called Harold Horsfall. He's one of the planning officers.'

'I'll check it,' said Colley and walked into the hall. Everyone could hear him talking on his mobile phone.

'I cannot believe that you would even suspect that one of us would kill Dennis,' said Margaret when he had gone.

'I didn't say I did. I merely—'

'Oh, don't play games, Inspector. Just tell me this, why would we do it? My husband's death does not benefit any of us. The company went into liquidation and we were left with nothing, and well you know it.'

'Nothing except this nice house.' Blizzard looked round the room with its antiques and the grandfather clock ticking gently in a corner. 'Hardly call it nothing.'

'Mortgaged to the hilt and, before you say it, no, Dennis did not have a life assurance policy. He did not believe in them.'

Colley walked back into the room and glanced apologetically at Blizzard. 'Harold Horsfall has confirmed that Robert was with him.'

'In which case,' said Blizzard, 'we have to consider who else could have assaulted Dennis.'

'Who on earth would want to?' asked Margaret.

'You people just don't get it, do you?' said Blizzard, unable to conceal his irritation. 'I'm not sure any of you are safe. Indeed, my sergeant tells me that the factory was hit again last night.'

'Kids,' snorted Robert. 'What happened when the factory closed was unfortunate but—'

'Unfortunate?' said Blizzard, not noticing his sergeant closing his eyes. 'Those people trusted you and—'

'Perhaps you should leave us to our grief now,' said Margaret, standing up.

'Not that easy,' said Blizzard. The door opened to reveal a man in his thirties, his brown wavy hair beautifully groomed, his grey designer suit with its blue silk tie immaculate and his black shoes gleaming. Behind him, they could see several other figures in the hallway. 'This is Detective Inspector Ross. He and his colleagues will conduct a thorough forensic examination of the house.'

'Oh, for fuck's sake!' exclaimed Robert.

Twenty-five minutes later, Colley walked out of the front door and down the drive to where Blizzard was leaning against his car, watching the gardener clipping the hedges.

'You checked him?' asked the inspector.

'This isn't Agatha Christie.' Noticing Blizzard's irritable look, the sergeant nodded. 'Sorry. Yes, I've checked him. Seems he was on a week off. Bridlington with his sister.'

'We sure?'

'Can't you see his suntan? Besides, who would make up a visit to Bridlington at this time of year? Anyway, there was a postcard on the fridge. I'll double-check it with the B & B when we get back.'

'OK.' Blizzard got into the driver's seat and started the engine. He looked back at the house. 'They're hiding something.'

'The only thing they appear to be hiding,' said the sergeant, lowering himself into the passenger's seat and glancing down at the receipts in his hand, 'is how much the women spend on shoes. According to this, they shelled out four hundred and eighty-six quid at Jarratts.'

'And they say crime doesn't pay,' murmured Blizzard, glancing at the two double garages. The door of one of them was open, revealing a Jaguar and a Bentley. Both appeared to be new.

'Assuming what they've done *is* a crime,' said Colley.

'You sound like Arthur.'

'You're the one who says follow the evidence and we didn't find any, did we?'

'Ah, but that's not the point, is it?' said Blizzard, edging the car down the drive. 'What am I always saying?'

'I've already quoted one of your little sayings; isn't one enough?'

'Humour me.'

'Not the one about it not being the truth that matters?' hazarded Colley.

'Precisely. It's what people assume to be true that matters. Remember when that vicar had his windows put out because the locals thought he was a paedophile? Didn't matter that he was innocent.'

'You gone away from it being one of the family, then?'

'They have all got alibis.'

'One of the workers?'

Blizzard edged the car out onto the country road, proceeding cautiously because the entrance to the drive was on a blind bend.

'Maybe,' he said. 'Those guys at The Red Lion that young Katie keeps mentioning, for instance. Garland and his little friends?'

'You want to lift them? See what they know?'

'Not yet. Don't want anything to spook tonight. Hey, we're only five minutes from my place, do you mind if we pop home for a moment and check how Fee is?'

'I'm sure she'll be delighted,' said Colley. 'Hey, you can make her a cup of coffee. She'll love that.'

Chapter Seven

'T HE ANSWER'S IN there somewhere,' said Blizzard, placing a fading newspaper cutting on his desk, next to his mug of tea. 'I'm sure of it.'

The inspector looked at the three detectives sitting opposite him and jabbed a finger on the front-page story with its bold, three-deck headline:

FURY AS HISTORIC FIRM
REACHES THE END
OF THE ROAD

The black and white image accompanying the story showed a line of uniformed officers shepherding four grim-faced people through a mob of angry workers gathered outside the Smarts factory on the day the closure was announced.

Leading the way, Dennis Smart was trying to ignore the shouting as he hurried towards his Jaguar and, beside him, half-hidden by a burly constable, his wife looked frightened. Blizzard looked at her with interest; in all the times he had confronted Margaret Smart, it was the first time he had seen her calm demeanour ruffled, ever seen her look like she cared. It was one of the things that had always disturbed the inspector, the way none of the four directors ever seemed to consider the men and women they had thrown on the jobs scrapheap, the lives they had wrecked by their actions, not just workers but local companies in the supply chain, family companies with proud, honest histories but who had been destroyed by greed.

In the wake of the closure, it was estimated that the suppliers had been owed the thick end of £5 million between them and Blizzard had used the suspicion that the Smarts directors had defaulted on the payments in order to siphon off the cash as justification to involve Western Division's Fraud Squad. The chief inspector had been angered by what had happened. It seemed to him a serious injustice and he sympathized with the views expressed by the protestors. He himself knew of four workers' marriages which had broken up over the strain of it all and there had also been rumours of a suicide, a supplier who had gone into his office one night and swallowed an overdose of sleeping pills, but no one ever seemed able to pin down the facts. The story persisted even though Blizzard had come to doubt its veracity.

Just in front of the couple captured on the photograph, and furiously hurling profanities back at the workers, was a jowly, balding man identified in the caption as George Rawcliffe. The picture suggested that he was in the process of sticking two fingers up at the workers and his face was twisted with anger, spittle flying from his lips. Lagging slightly behind the others, with a knowing smile on his face, was a dark-haired young man in a sharp suit worn under an expensive camel-hair coat. The caption said that his name was Jason Heavens. Blizzard stared at him; Heavens was always the director who had fascinated him the most. Smart and Rawcliffe he understood; crude-mouthed bullies who had blustered their way through their interviews as detectives investigated the stories of missing cash. Margaret was someone with pretensions of her own importance and came over as a lesser player in the racket, but Heavens was urbane, calm, self-contained. He had given nothing away in the interviews and had always worn that knowing smile. Despite his irritation, Blizzard had found himself intrigued by the man.

'So here's your starter for ten,' said the inspector, looking at the photograph. 'Smart's murder suggests we may need to reappraise things. Are they suspects or victims?'

'Victims,' said Colley immediately. 'One down, three to go.'

'Versace?' asked Blizzard, looking at Graham Ross.

'Victims,' nodded Ross; the divisional head of forensics had only just returned to Abbey Road, his examination of Larch House having failed to throw up anything of interest. He gestured to the crowd of furious workers in the picture. 'I reckon your killer is one of them. They've got plenty of motive. And plenty of anger to go with it.'

'Motive, yes,' said Blizzard, 'but anger? That picture was taken eight months ago. Have people not moved on?'

'Maybe some of them have but the anger has not died down, has it?' said the third officer. 'It's still as raw as ever, as you keep reminding us.'

Chris Ramsey was one of the Division's two detective inspectors: the organizer, the one who drew up the rosters and allocated the manpower. A slim, tall man with short-cropped brown hair, he had an angular face, a prominent nose and a thin mouth not given to laughing. Although Ramsey was, in Blizzard's opinion, a detective with little imagination, the DCI had long since come to value his judgement and he sought it now.

'So you coming down on the side of victims as well, Chris?' he asked.

'Definitely,' nodded Ramsey. 'It's just a question of who's next, I'm afraid.'

'Why be afraid?' said Blizzard. 'They've got it coming to them, all of them.'

Robert Smart looked across at his mother, who was sitting in her usual armchair in the living room.

'I've asked Henry Gallen to move our money,' he said.

'Are you sure that's wise? The police didn't find it last time, why should they do so now?'

'I told you,' said Robert, coming to sit next to her. 'I don't trust Blizzard. And now that it's a murder inquiry, he's got all the excuse he needs to come after us. No amount of complaining to the chief constable will stop him.'

'What did Henry say when you asked him to do it? You seemed to think that he's getting cold feet about the whole thing.'

'Henry Gallen will do as he's told. He knows what will happen if he doesn't.'

'Just so long as you trust him,' said his mother.

Robert did not reply. His silence spoke volumes.

'Maybe it's not that simple, though,' said Blizzard. 'Maybe it's not about revenge, after all. Never heard of a falling-out among thieves? They siphon the money off when the factory closes down but now there's been some sort of split. Wouldn't exactly be the first time we've seen it happen over money, would it?'

'Granted,' replied Colley, 'but if you're right, it's got to be Rawcliffe or Heavens. Like you yourself said, the family all have alibis.'

'Alibis can be faked.'

'Not these ones. The shoe shop has confirmed that the women's receipt is genuine, and, anyway one of the assistants remembered them going in. Said Margaret looked down her nose at her the whole time. And as for Robert, that council guy seemed pretty adamant that he was there. And it's in the visitors' book. I nipped over to check.'

'So it's Rawcliffe or Heavens, then.' Blizzard tapped the newspaper picture. 'Neither of them are particularly edifying human beings and Rawcliffe and Dennis Smart definitely did not get on, from what I heard. Lots of arguments when they ran the factory. I'm not sure the relationship with Heavens was much better. And we don't know where either of them was when Dennis was attacked, remember.'

'Sorry, but I think it's still more likely to be one of the workers,' said Ramsey, gesturing to the image. 'Look at the crowd, guv, just look at those faces.'

'I agree,' said Colley. 'I bumped into Lenny Capelli; he was one of the police officers on duty that day, that's him at the end of line trying to hold that fat bloke back. Lenny reckons it's the scariest job he's ever done. Reckons it was a miracle no one got hurt.'

The sergeant pointed to one of the workers, a wild-haired man with his face twisted as he shouted obscenities, his clenched fist waved just inches from a police officer's face.

'That's Baz Garland,' he said. 'He organized the protest. Not sure he even worked there, mind. He's one of those troublemakers who latch themselves onto anything going.'

Colley winked at the others as he watched Blizzard lean further over to peer at the picture, struggling to make out the finer details.

'I don't mean to be rude,' said the sergeant, 'but isn't Fee right? Isn't it time you got some specs?'

'I guess,' said Blizzard, straightening up with a rueful look on his face. 'Not sure I will be able to read bedtime stories to the little 'un without them.'

Colley glanced at the clock and shook his head at the others. Nowhere near the record, said his expression. Blizzard noticed the look but said nothing. Sometimes, he reasoned, you just had to let these things go. If he was honest, part of him enjoyed the good-humoured ribbing that the impending arrival had engendered.

Besides, thought the inspector, he was changing; he had resisted the idea at first but could see it clearly now. Ever since Fee had told him that she was pregnant, he had found himself becoming less judgemental, more understanding. He'd seen it with others once they became parents; hard-driven officers whose priorities changed, who did not work the hours they did previously, who reacted differently to events. Who were somehow more *human*. The old John Blizzard, he suspected, would not have been so personally affected by the plight of the men and women who had lost their jobs at Smarts that bleak winter morning.

Noticing the others looking at him uneasily, he gave a wry smile.

'Sorry, boys,' he said. 'That whisky's still going to the girl in the canteen, I'm afraid.'

The others laughed, partly with relief; you never knew how John Blizzard would react.

'What I was looking at,' continued the inspector, looking once more at the cutting and tapping a man standing at the back of the crowd, his face twisted with hatred like the others, 'is this feller. I seem to recognize him, just not sure why.'

Ramsey also leaned over to look closer.

'Edward,' he said, furrowing his brow, 'Edward, Edward. Fothergill, I think that's it. Ran a little engineering firm, three or four guys and his wife doing the admin. Went bust because Smarts owed them three quarters of a million, as I recall. He cropped up in the original inquiry.'

Blizzard nodded. 'I met him, I think. He came in to see the Fraud Squad. In tears, he was. Blamed the Smarts for wrecking his business. Maybe worth checking him out, we're going to have to cast the net wide on this one and we need to start somewhere. We'll need a list of all the suppliers.'

'I'll sort that,' said Ramsey.

'And I'll go and see Fothergill,' said Colley.

'Wait until tonight's done and dusted,' said Blizzard. 'I want to play it low key until we get the fun and games at the Lion over.'

'You still want us to lift Garland and his pals tonight, though?' asked Ramsey. 'I mean, when we're in there?'

'Yeah, but let them think it's wrong place, wrong time. Hardly anyone knows that Robert Smart was murdered and I want to keep it that way for the moment. In the meantime, I want to know where Rawcliffe and Heavens are.' Blizzard glanced at the clock again. Four p.m. 'OK, gents, don't let me keep you. Besides, I've got someone coming in from the kindergarten.'

Once out in the corridor, Ramsey looked at Colley and Ross with a bemused expression on his face.

'Kindergarten?' he asked. 'We setting up a créche?'

'Would we were,' grinned Ross. A slim young man wearing a dark suit and carrying a briefcase appeared at the far end of the corridor and started walking towards them. 'Ah, there he is now.'

'Jesus,' murmured Ramsey. 'Has Fee popped the sprog?'
Colley roared with laughter.

Alison Rutter left the nursing home shortly after 4 p.m.
walking with slow and heavy tread towards her car. Even
though she had been a nurse for six years, and had seen
more people die than she cared to count, she still found
visiting her grandfather an excruciating ordeal. It was
different when it was one of your own, she realized that,
and every time she went to see the old man, every time she
looked down at his hunched and twisted shape sitting in
his customary chair in the corner of the lounge, every time
she stared into those lifeless eyes, listened to the rasping
of his breathing, she felt the tears welling up.

The visits were increasingly brief. Alf Webb's condition
had deteriorated rapidly since he had been admitted to
the home two months previously when his arthritis-ridden
wife found herself unable to cope with the ravages of his
asbestosis. The big strong man with the insatiable love of
life, the mischievous sense of humour and the infectious
laugh had long gone, replaced by a husk of a human being
who did not appear to recognize any of his loved ones or
even realize where he was.

This visit had been no different for Alison and, after
twenty minutes in which no words were uttered, her
grandfather curled up as usual in his chair, she had taken
her leave. Fighting back the tears, she got into her car
and drove out of the cul-de-sac, heading for the General
Hospital and her night shift. As the Mini drove past
a parked grey Ford, Alison did not notice how its driver
slunk down in the seat, not re-emerging into view until
she was long gone.

Nick Towler got out of the car, glanced up the road to

make sure no one had seen him and gave a sigh of relief; it would not have done for her to have identified him, although he was pretty sure she did not know he was a cop anyway. Blizzard had been insistent that they kept things as low key as possible during their initial inquiries into the death of Dennis Smart.

Once at the front of the home, the detective constable rang the bell and, after a minute or so, the door was opened by one of the staff.

The officer flashed his warrant card.

'DC Towler from Abbey Road,' he said. 'Can I see the manager, please?'

The late-afternoon light was already fading when George Rawcliffe sped along the dual carriageway taking him east into Hafton. When he reached the fringes of the city, back in familiar surroundings for the first time in six months, he turned off up a slip road and crossed the bridge to drop down onto the old service route created for the warehouses that had once been ranged along the northern bank of the river. The warehouses had long gone, victims of recession, and, after driving through the wasteland for a couple of hundred metres, Rawcliffe turned onto a narrow tarmacked track, the vehicle's tyres crunching on gravel as its headlights cut a swathe through the gathering gloom. The Merc came to a halt in a small car-park at the water's edge.

Rawcliffe cut the engine and got out. Walking down to the water, he stared across the Haft towards the lights of the chemical complex on the south side. Seeing nothing of beauty in the reflections off the water, Rawcliffe scowled as he recalled his days working at the plant as a young engineer, toiling away between the stacks and the chimneys, hating the people with whom he worked, resenting their cruel comments about his broad Yorkshire accent and dreaming of the day he would be rich. The day he would leave them all behind. The day he would be *somebody*.

Well, that day had come, he thought with relish. Stamping his feet to keep warm in the late-afternoon chill that was blowing raw off the choppy waters, Rawcliffe glanced back at the black Merc, which had been purchased just a few days previously. With cash. He allowed himself a smug smile as he recalled the showroom assistant's expression when he produced the money. Yes, despite all that had happened, despite the collapse of Smarts and the awkward questions from Blizzard and that sergeant of his, Rawcliffe knew that he was still someone to be envied. He had achieved everything he wanted. He was all right, always had been, always would be. Money no object. No one got the better of George Rawcliffe, especially not some flat-footed cop. Nevertheless, for all his confidence, Rawcliffe had felt it prudent to leave the city as soon as possible after the factory closure; too many threats, too many late-night phone calls, too many difficult questions from John Blizzard in that last interview.

This was the first time he had been back since it all blew up and, had he not been summoned by the call that morning, he would not have returned; grimy little Hafton was in his past now and he was only in the city again with the utmost reluctance. Rawcliffe reached into his coat pocket and brought out a packet of cigarettes. He fished a lighter from another pocket, lit a cigarette and stood for a few moments, savouring the aroma as the smoke curled its way up into the darkening evening air.

On hearing the crunch of shoes on the gravel, he turned and saw a figure emerge from a clump of trees down by the riverside.

'Why we meeting here?' Rawcliffe asked the man. 'Bit dramatic, ain't it? And what's so important that it can't be done on the phone? Do you how far I've driven to—?'

'You talked to Heavens?'

'Rang him after you called. He agrees that the old bastard will not be missed.'

'You'll not be missed either.'

Rawcliffe saw that the figure had produced a gun from the folds of his coat. A silencer had been fitted to the barrel.

'What the...?'

'Assuming they ever find your fat carcass, that is,' sneered the man. 'You'll probably sink straight to the bottom.' He pointed the gun at Rawcliffe. 'Time to pay some debts, Georgie boy. I know what you did. Turn round.'

'What?'

'Turn round.'

'If this is a piss-t—'

'I'm serious, Georgie boy.' The man gave a slight smile. 'Deadly serious. Now, turn round, there's a good boy.'

'If it's money you want—'

'I don't want money, George. See, I know what you did to Amy.'

'You can't prove nothing!'

'Ah, but I can.'

Rawcliffe snapped out a meaty hand but his assailant was quicker and the gun smashed into his face, cracking bone and sending him reeling backwards, blood flying, to sink to his knees on the gravel, his vision blurred, his head spinning. After a few seconds, Rawcliffe staggered to his feet and shook his head but when his eyesight cleared, the clearing was empty. Rawcliffe peered closer but could not see his attacker anywhere. He gave a nervous laugh.

'Always were a fucking coward,' he said. 'You run, you run like a stuck—'

Which was when he heard the scrape of a boot behind him. He did not even have time to cry out and no one heard the muffled thud of the shot or the splash a few moments later as his body was dragged into the Haft to float gently downstream. No one saw the figure disappear into the trees either. Or so it seemed.

Chapter Eight

IF THERE WAS one thing guaranteed to make John Blizzard feel his age, particularly given that he was well into his final decade as a serving police officer, it was young coppers. And if there was one thing guaranteed to irritate him, it was smart-arse young coppers who thought they they had all the answers. In fact, the inspector noted gloomily as he glanced down at the card that the young man had slid across the desk, Martin Bartholomew was not even a police officer. Probably not old enough, thought the inspector.

'This doesn't give your rank,' said the inspector grumpily. 'You not a cop, then?'

'I'm a civilian, sir. I came to the Fraud Squad on a placement from Hafton University last month.'

'University?' Blizzard stared suspiciously at the remnants of acne on Bartholomew's face and the lank black hair which looked like it had not been washed for days. 'This is a murder inquiry, sunshine, what good is some kid fresh from—?'

'A lot of good, actually, sir.' Bartholomew seemed unruffled by the inspector's ire. 'You see, not only did I graduate with a first in Economics but I also studied for the best part of two years under Professor Meehan.'

Blizzard looked blank.

'Professor Roy Meehan,' explained Bartholomew. 'He's a world expert in criminology, especially the emergence of electronic fraud. That's what I wrote my thesis on, in fact. I'm developing my ideas in my Masters.'

'Your thesis! Masters! Jesus, when your gaffer said he was sending someone to help I had no idea he was talking about some kid who's wet behind the ears.'

'Please don't underestimate me, sir. I really can help you with this Smarts business, you know. In fact, I'll be much more useful than any of your detectives.'

'What on earth does that mean?' said the inspector, glowering at him. 'If you are suggesting that my highly trained—'

'Electronic crime is a rapidly developing branch of criminal activity and it is crucial that, as a force, you embrace new forms of less traditional policing in order to ensure that we facilitate its detection.'

'Facilitate?' snapped the inspector, irritated at the way he had been interrupted. John Blizzard was not used to being interrupted and he did not like people who used words like facilitate. 'You're not in the sodding classroom now.'

The inspector stood up and walked over to open the door.

'And I don't need a lecture from some smart-arse kid either,' he said, gesturing towards the corridor. 'So, since I have a lot of "traditional" police work to be getting on with, might I suggest that you sling your hook and get your sorry—?'

'I've found the money.'

Blizzard looked at him in amazement for a few moments then closed the door and sat back down behind the desk slowly.

'You've done what?' he said.

'I've found the money that the Smarts directors siphoned off from the business.'

'So I was right, then?'

'Not about me, you weren't.'

Blizzard considered the comment for a moment and nodded; despite his famed ill temper, the inspector had always respected people who were prepared to speak up for themselves. Didn't always like it but respected the fact that they had done it all the same. Besides, on this occasion the inspector was overwhelmed by an uncomfortable sense of having been outmanoeuvred by someone less than half his age who had an unnerving amount of self-confidence.

'I guess I did misjudge you,' said the DCI grudgingly. He gave Bartholomew a rueful look. 'Us dinosaurs tend to take a bit of convincing, you see. So tell me more about the money.'

'Well, when DI Raymond heard that Dennis Smart might die, he had an inkling that you would ask the Fraud Squad to take another look at the case so he asked me to review the evidence. All on the QT, of course.'

'And you found the money?'

'And I found the money.'

'Where?'

'In a pillowcase under Dennis Smart's bed. God knows how no one found it when they searched the house.'

Blizzard stared at him.

'Joke,' said Bartholomew hurriedly, noticing the expression and cursing the way he had tried to be clever; Colley had warned him about overconfidence when it came to John Blizzard. 'Sorry, sir. Poor taste. No, they'd worked hard to conceal it but if you know where to look, you can usually follow the trail well enough.'

'If it's that easy, how come Fraud Squad didn't find it before, then?' grunted the inspector. 'The buggers spent months looking without turning up so much as a brass farthing.'

'Like I said, sir, electronic fraud is a rapidly developing field and most police forces are way behind when it comes to handling it. And to be fair, the Smarts directors were very clever.'

'They don't come over as clever,' said Blizzard, glancing down at the newspaper cutting still sitting on the desk with the picture of Rawcliffe about to stick two fingers up at the baying mob.

"Which is why I reckon that they must have had help. Whoever it was knew exactly what they were doing. Used several different accounts under several different names before their money turned up in Liechtenstein.'

'Liechtenstein?'

'It's between Switzerland and Austria.'

'Yes, thank you, I know where it is.' Blizzard gave a rueful smile. 'Actually, I don't. Live and learn, eh?'

Bartholomew returned the smile tentatively; like everyone said, you just did not know where you stood with John Blizzard and he'd heard the stories about the chief inspector's outbursts.

'So, does that mean all the money is in the same place?' asked the DCI. 'In Liechtenstein?'

'Not all of it. Just that belonging to Dennis and his wife, as far as I can see. It took a bit of doing to find the rest of it but I finally tracked Rawcliffe's down to Miami and Heavens seems to have deposited his in the Cayman Islands.'

'This accountant who helped them ... I assume it must have been an accountant?' said the inspector and Bartholomew nodded. 'Any way of narrowing it down?'

'I can do better than that, sir. According to your sergeant, you're interested in a guy called Henry Gallen?'

'He was the company accountant. Got very rich very quickly, hence our interest. Trouble is, we couldn't turn up anything to link him to criminal activity.'

'Well, I just happen to know Henry Gallen. He was one of Professor Meehan's students at the university. Came to one of his night classes four or five years back. About electronic fraud.'

'Now, that *is* interesting.' Blizzard sat back and surveyed the young man with renewed respect. 'You're quite a piece of work, Mr Bartholomew. Tell me, how much money are we talking about here? Tens of thousands? A hundred thousand maybe?'

'I think not, sir.'

'Aye, I guess it *was* only a small company.'

'It was small for a reason, though. Smarts would have been considerably larger had the directors not diverted the profits into their own pockets instead of declaring it to the taxman. They'd been doing it for years, from what I can see.'

'So how much are we talking about?'

Bartholomew clipped open his briefcase and produced several pieces of paper.

'As far as I can deduce,' he said, glancing down, 'Dennis and Margaret Smart creamed more than nineteen million off the business and Rawcliffe and Heavens pocketed near enough ten each over the same period. Just shy of forty million in total, give or take.'

'Forty million?' Blizzard gaped at him. 'You sure?'

Bartholomew slid the pieces of paper across the desk.

'See for yourself,' he said.

'Jesus, that's a lot of cash,' said Blizzard, as he scanned the figures, acutely aware that he could not read them and that, even if he could, he would struggle to interpret them anyway. Mathematics had never been his strong point. His expenses sheets were always being sent back by Accounts with red lines round the queries. Now he shook his head at the numbers. 'People kept saying they were bent but folks wouldn't listen.'

'You listened,' said Bartholomew, clipping closed his briefcase and standing up.

Blizzard nodded. 'Yes, I did,' he said. 'Strike one for traditional policing, eh?'

Ten minutes later, the inspector was sitting in his office, deep in thought, his feet up on the desk, when there was a knock on the door and Nick Towler walked in.

'You come up with anything?' asked the inspector, lowering his feet and gesturing to a chair.

'Yeah,' nodded the detective constable, sitting down. 'The manager was not very pleased but I told her she'd be charged with obstruction if she did not let me in. And I told her to keep shtoom about my visit.'

Blizzard nodded approvingly. 'What did you find out, then?'

'The old feller's been there for a couple of months. They let me see him but I don't think he even knew I was there. He's in a right state. Mind, they all are. Remind me not to get old.'

'Indeed,' said Blizzard.

Chapter Nine

DARKNESS HAD LONG since fallen when the police teams started to gather in the briefing room at Abbey Road, the atmosphere crackling with the excitement of taking part in a John Blizzard raid. There had not been one on this scale for several months, not since they had broken up that drugs network operating out of the old food-processing factory at the back of the football stadium, and the thought of settling old scores at The Red Lion had captured imaginations and given the event an extra frisson. Many of the officers now streaming into the room had volunteered to come in on their days off. No one wanted to miss an event which they believed would go down in Abbey Road legend.

They also knew that the operation formed part of a deliberate strategy. Many of those gathered recalled that, before they had embarked on the drugs raid in May, the DCI had given one of his robust briefings in the same room, stressing repeatedly that the police were still a force to be reckoned with in Hafton, whatever the villains were saying. That the streets did not belong to the criminals. It was the inspector's mantra, one he shared with Arthur Ronald.

Before the two men had been reunited at Western Division, many officers, uniformed and plainclothes, had found themselves increasingly disillusioned, overwhelmed by a sense that the police were impotent in the face of criminal activity and robbed of confidence that their senior officers possessed the strength of character to redress the imbalance. However, with their insistence that doors go in and go in hard, Ronald and Blizzard had changed all that. Ignore the snipings from the media, forget the tauntings of the villains, they had said, the streets of the city belong to the police and always would.

The approach brought about rewards and the operation in May had illustrated the point. Each officer had left the briefing room feeling ten feet tall and the raid had been a great success as, inspired by the inspector's rousing words, the teams smashed their way into the factory, made eleven arrests and seized £250,000 of smack. What was just as important was the impact on public perception; everyone knew that Blizzard hated the media but that few played the game better and the next day's evening paper was full of pictures of struggling suspects being manhandled out of the old factory. Like Blizzard always said, 'There are few better police officers than a good headline.' Another of his sayings.

However, that had been four months ago and everyone in Abbey Road had sensed for some weeks that the time had come for a repeat performance. So, one by one, officers filtered into the briefing room, filling it with talk and laughter and an underlying tension despite their excitement. No one was under any illusion that a raid on the pub was different, that it could cause trouble if you got it wrong. A lot of trouble. Trouble like few others.

The pub had a long-standing and notorious reputation, not just for thievery but also for a few hotheads who had little time for the police and did not care who knew it.

Men like Baz Garland. Men with mouths on them and the capacity to turn violent. Each officer knew that the reaction was likely to be volatile. Many of those gathered in the briefing room remembered the winter's night nine years previously when two detective constables went in to carry out a routine arrest only to be forced out under a barrage of bottles, one of them nursing a gashed face and a broken nose after being attacked by several men wielding pool cues. It had taken the riot teams three and a half hours to quieten the situation down as the trouble spilled out onto the street. A subsequent search of the pub discovered an undischarged firearm behind the bar and four knives.

The Red Lion had issued its warning and people still recalled the event the best part of a decade later, partly because it had long-lasting ramifications. In the wake of what the local newspaper had dubbed the Battle of Haverton Street, the police tried to have the pub closed down at a licensing hearing but the brewery escaped with a warning from the bench even though the district commander submitted a meticulously compiled dossier of violent incidents dealt with by his officers. Things had been quieter in recent times but the bench's decision still rankled with officers, none more so than the man sent by his commander to represent the police at the hearing, then uniformed chief inspector Arthur Ronald. Everyone knew that Ronald was frustrated by the fact that The Red Lion remained open.

Further along the corridor from the briefing room, Blizzard sat in his office, feet on desk again and idly flicking a pen round in his fingers, the lull in the day's activities having allowed his mind to stray to his argument with Fee that morning, if indeed it was an argument; he was not quite sure. Never was. One moment she would be biting his head off, the next demanding affection. He had rung her several times but she did not answer, fuelling his uncertainty. He hoped she was not ignoring his calls. The inspector had found himself contemplating such things more and more in recent months, his mind weighed down with the responsibilities of impending fatherhood, something he had never thought he would experience, especially not after his first marriage as a young man blew apart amid such acrimony.

It was with relief that the inspector was able to banish such thoughts, lowering his feet to the floor as Arthur Ronald walked in.

'Now then,' said Blizzard as the superintendent sat down.

'Thought I'd check where we are with the Smart inquiry. I hear Fraud Squad have turned up the missing cash.' Ronald gave a rueful half-smile. 'Good call. Perhaps you are infallible, after all, John.'

'Modesty forbids me from commenting.'

'For which praise be. Any word on Rawcliffe and Heavens?'

'Last we heard, Rawcliffe was living on the outskirts of Birmingham. The local bobbies did a quick drive past his house this afternoon and reckon that no one was in. Bankrupt or not, he seems to have hung on to plenty of cash. The Brummie boys reckon his gaff is worth a couple of mill. Mock Tudor. Typical of the man. They're going to keep an eye on it for us.'

'And Heavens?'

'Who knows about the fragrant Jason? We still reckon he's in Spain. I've got Interpol checking their files again, see if they've turned anything up since we asked last time.' The inspector glanced at the clock: 7.15. 'You want to take the briefing?'

'No,' said Ronald, standing up and heading for the door. 'You do it so much more, how shall we say it, theatrically? Just make sure we get enough to close the bloody place down, yes? Ah, Constable Summers. You might be about to make an old man very happy.'

'Thank you, sir,' said Summers as the superintendent lumbered past her and into the corridor. She remained by the door even when he had gone and looked timidly at Blizzard. 'You wanted to see me, sir?'

'Yes, I did. Don't stand on ceremony, pull up a pew.' Blizzard gave her what he hoped was a reassuring smile. 'Oh, and close the door.'

'Have I done anything wrong?' she asked, shutting the door and sitting down.

'Wrong?' He noticed her anxious expression; he really must work on that smile. 'What makes you think that you've done anything wrong?'

She hesitated. 'You do have a bit of a reputation for being a bit ... well, fierce.'

'Fierce? Do you know what I spent part of last weekend doing, Constable?'

She shook her head.

'Choosing teddy bears at Toys R Us, that's what. Me and the missus. Mind, I quite liked Barney. The purple dinosaur, you know?' He glanced at the clock. 'Twenty-eight seconds. Do you like whisky, by any chance, Constable Summers?'

'Sir?'

'No need to look so worried. I'm very pleased with the work you've done at the Lion. Not sure I'd fancy spending a month among all those scuzzballs.'

Summers gave a sigh of relief. The only previous time

she had met the DCI, he had been businesslike, not particularly warm, much more focused on ensuring that she was capable of working undercover, his questions clipped and short, his eyes never leaving her. Colley had since confided that intimidating people through eye contact was one of Blizzard's specialities. Certainly, during their meeting, the inspector had left the warmth to Colley; she had assumed that was the way they worked. The old good cop, bad cop routine. Summers had left the meeting with a sense of excitement at what was to come but also foreboding at working for such a strict taskmaster. Now, here was the legendary John Blizzard making jokes about purple dinosaurs.

'If I'm not in trouble, why do you want to see me?' she asked, trying to make sense of what was happening.

'How do you fancy a transfer? Over here, to work for me at Abbey Road?'

'Me, sir?'

'This was not an easy assignment, Constable. In fact, it was a pretty crappy one and you have shown yourself very capable, very capable indeed. Colley speaks very highly of you as well and my governor's been after the Lion for years so he's chuffed to bits.'

'Is that what Mr Ronald meant by making him happy?'

Blizzard nodded. 'This is the nearest we have got to closing the place down for years. If you did come over here, you couldn't go undercover again, of course, too many folks know your face now, but I am sure we could find you something equally as challenging. Got to be more exciting than looking for rabbit poachers.'

'But what about my boss? DCI—'

'You leave your gaffer to us. The big question first is do you want to come and work for me?'

Summers thought of the wild looks of Baz Garland in the corner of the snug, remembered the lowlifes in the bedsits, recalled the stranger standing outside the shop when she had left that morning, thought of the peace of her rural beat, thought of....

'I'm not sure,' she said slowly. 'It's a big jump from Lincolnshire.'

'Maybe so but I'm a Yellowbelly as well. Lived there as a kid then came over here with my dad's work. Hated it at first but I got used to it after a while. Believe it or not, Hafton's got a somewhat dubious charm. And we go out of our way to look after our people here. What do you say?'

'Can I have time to think it over, please?'

'Of course.'

She searched his face for signs of irritation, half-expecting an outburst, but found nothing. 'Thank you,' she said. 'Was there anything else?'

'Yes. You've probably heard that Dennis Smart's death turns out to be murder?'

'The sarge told me, yes, sir. I assume you want to know if Baz Garland and his mates are capable of doing it.'

'I know I said that they're pissheads but they're angry pissheads and ones with reason enough to hate Dennis Smart. I need to know if they are angry enough to have killed him. Particularly Baz Garland: he's a real hothead, that one.'

'I certainly think he's capable of murder.'

'You don't think he's just a gobshite?'

She shook her head. 'He's wild.'

'I was afraid you might say that,' sighed Blizzard, walking over to the window and staring out into the gathering darkness. 'He's certainly got a record for violence. Maybe I misjudged him. And the others? Did I get them wrong as well?'

'Tommy Webb does seem to look up to Garland but I'm not convinced that he would follow him in something like that. Mind, he does blame the company for his father's illness.'

'If it was my dad, I'd be angry as well. And Ron Maskell? The soft lad? He up to killing anyone?'

'Not sure he even knows what day it is.'

'They're the most dangerous ones,' said the inspector gloomily. He turned back from the window and sat down at his desk. 'The ones who'll do what they're told. We'll definitely need to lift them all tonight.'

'Can I go along?'

'Not sure it's a good idea. God knows how they'll react when they see you. Not sure we want to inflame things more than we have to.'

'I can handle it, sir. And you'll need someone to point out faces.'

Blizzard looked at her eager expression.

'If you really want to,' he said, 'and as long as you know what you're getting yourself into. And stop calling me sir. That's for uniform. Go on, on your way.'

She grinned, stood up and headed for the door. 'Yes, guv.'

'That's better. Oh, before you go, I understand you think that you've been watched?'

Summers looked anxious again, her hand on the door handle.

'I did tell the sarge straight away,' she said, 'and it was probably only my imagination—'

'Far from it.' Blizzard turned to look out of the window again. 'It just shows what a good officer you are that you clocked him.'

'I hope I haven't ruined the operation. I tried my best to make sure that I....' Her voiced tailed away and she looked at him in bewilderment. 'Hang on, did you know I was being followed?'

'Oh, aye. He's called Jimmy Grainer. Jimbo to his friends. Not that he has many.'

'Is he a criminal?'

'Actually, he's a DC we borrowed from the East side. It was a risk but not many people over this side of the city know him. We didn't say anything to you because it would have changed the way you behaved and they're canny in the Lion. I'll have to have a word with him about being clocked, mind. Dozy bastard.'

'Why was he watching me?'

'There was no way we were going to let you go in alone. Like I said, we look after our people here.'

There was a knock on the door and Nick Towler walked in.

'Sorry to interrupt, guv,' he said, 'but Traffic have just been on. One of their patrols spotted Rawcliffe's car heading into Hafton on the motorway. Trouble is, they were on the westbound carriageway and by the time they turned round, it had disappeared.'

'Returning to the scene of the crime,' murmured Blizzard. 'I wonder which one, though?'

Chapter Ten

'NOT SEEN YOU for a while,' said Tommy Webb as he walked into the snug to find a scruffy young man sitting behind the bar, reading the newspaper.

'Got behind with me studies. Shouldn't be here really but they rang in a panic.'

'Where's the blonde bird?'

'Ally?' said the barman, glancing up from the sports pages. 'She called in sick, mate.'

'Pity, I like her.'

'I'm sure you do,' said the young man, watching as Garland and Maskell took their seats at their normal table in the corner. 'What'll it be, then?'

'Three pints,' said Webb. 'What's wrong with her, then?'

'Food poisoning, I think. Rang in this morning, apparently.' He glanced at a large jar sitting on the end of the bar. 'Probably one of Doug's pickled eggs that done it. They've been there since 1976.'

'Yeah, probably,' grinned Webb. He waited for the barman to pour the drinks and carried the glasses back to the corner table where he placed them in front of Garland and Maskell. 'There you go, gents.'

'Where is she, then?' asked Garland.

'Kid reckons it's food poisoning.'

Garland shook his head. 'Na,' he said, 'there's something funny going on. She looked OK last night, Tommy.'

'Yeah, but these things come on quick, mind. I had it once after a bad curry. Two hours after we left the restaurant I was sick as a dog. Me and the missus.'

'Yeah, well, I still don't like it.' Garland stood up and reached for his coat. 'I'm off.'

'Relax, will you, man?' protested Webb. 'Sit down and drink your pint.'

Garland hesitated before eventually sitting down.

'We just got to be careful,' he said in a low voice, glancing around to make sure that he was not being overheard by the barman. 'The cops are bound to be all over this already.'

'Yeah, but they don't know nothing, Baz,' said Ron. 'And they don't know nothing about us.'

'Don't they? I heard that sergeant was up at the factory this morning, looking at where the fire was. That lad, runs the bike shop on the corner: he said the copper went in there as well, asking loads of questions. I tell you, we got to keep our heads down. And now that bird's gone off sick and....'

'She's just a kid.' protested Webb. 'I mean, what on earth can she know?'

Just before 7.30 p.m. with darkness deepening over Hafton, John Blizzard stood up and left his office to walk down the corridor, revelling as ever in the moments before he took the briefing. He had always loved briefings for big operations. Loved the sense of occasion, loved the way it seemed to bring out the best in him. The inspector believed that the commanding officers who forgot that this was a performance were the ones who failed to inspire when it really mattered. Blizzard remembered discussing the idea with Jay during an evening round at Colley's. The sergeant's girlfriend was a primary-school teacher and had agreed that the key to success was the ability to hold an audience, be they six-year-olds or forty-six-year-olds. 'Life is a performance, John,' she had said, sipping her red wine.

Which was why Blizzard always appreciated those moments before the performance began, before he stepped into the briefing room, relished the pounding of the heart, the rush of adrenalin, the acute awareness that it would be so easy to get it wrong. That last concern, the idea that it could go wrong, had not been a consideration for the inspector until recently. John Blizzard had always been a supremely confident police officer but with experience had come sneaking self-doubts, clammy hands and a voice that these days trembled slightly when he tried to evoke emotion in his audience. He wished it was not so but he realized yet again that impending fatherhood was changing him. Making him more vulnerable. And he did not like it. It got in the way of the job that needed to be done.

Banishing such thoughts with an irritable shake of the head, the inspector paused in the corridor, listening to the voices of the gathered officers, took a deep breath and strode into the packed briefing room where everyone watched him expectantly. From the front of the room, the inspector took a few moments to survey his audience, picking out Colley and Ramsey standing in their usual positions by the far wall, Nick Towler and Versace in the front row, Katie Summers next to them, her eyes shining with the excitement of it all; this was by far the biggest operation in which she had been involved.

The room was packed and, after giving a small nod of approval, Blizzard started his address, relieved that his voice sounded calm and measured.

'Ladies and gentlemen,' he said, 'thank you for your attendance. Before we start proceedings, I think we should pay tribute to the work of young Constable Summers here. Blame her for ruining your evening.'

A ripple of applause ran round the room and a couple of officers on the row behind Summers leaned forward and patted her on the back. She looked embarrassed, yet pleased.

'She also did it at great personal risk to herself,' continued the inspector gravely. 'Jesus, no one wants to be stalked by Jimmy Grainer.'

Laughter.

'So, given what she has done, make sure you don't balls it up tonight,' said Blizzard, voice suddenly hard. He did his usual trick of letting his gaze roam round the room, appearing to those in the audience to home in on them individually, a technique that had always made officers acutely conscious of their responsibilities. 'I want tonight to be nice and clean. No heroics. By the book. I don't want some fast-talking lawyer standing up in court and trying it on because we mucked it up. And I want them all as well. We've been after the Lion for too long to let any of them slip through our fingers now.'

Nods from the audience. Blizzard turned and gestured to the large board on which were pinned a dozen photographs. Several bull-faced, shaven-headed men, a few scrawny characters, a couple of flint-faced women with tattoos on their necks. Garland, Webb and Maskell were not on the board.

'This little lot of lovelies,' said the inspector, 'are the main ringleaders, according to the intelligence gathered by Constable Summers. You'll recognize a few of the faces,

I am sure. Most of them have got form for handling and at least four of them have done long stretches for burglary or robbery.'

A number of officers nodded once more. Book or not, Blizzard and Ronald were not the only ones who were out to settle old scores.

'A word of warning,' continued Blizzard. 'You do not, I am sure, need me to tell you about the crackerjacks who drink in the Lion. We all know what happened there nine years ago.'

He tapped one of the photographs.

'Jackie Gray is particularly handy with his fists, a long record of assaults and affray, and intelligence suggests that he may carry a knife these days.' The inspector glanced at the burly Support Group officers sitting together towards the back of the room. 'Which is why we have invited the heavy brigade along with us tonight. We'll go in when they've finished their pasties.'

Laughter rippled round the room and the Support Group officers grinned; one of them held up a Mars bar. Blizzard let the laughter die away naturally.

'And why the firearms boys are also here,' he continued solemnly, glancing this time at several officers standing over towards the window. 'It's not beyond the realms of possibility that some of the Lion's clientele will have firearms so we're taking no chances. OK. You will be briefed individually by your team leaders but before we go, I want to remind you that, there's a lot riding on this. I want to send a message out to the lowlifes and I don't want any fu—'

Blizzard stopped talking as Arthur Ronald walked into the room and took a seat by the door.

'Don't let me disturb you, John,' said the superintendent,

wafting a hand at his friend. 'You keep uttering profanities, son. Mind, not sure the baby will appreciate its dad cursing like a docker.' Ronald glanced at the clock on the wall. 'Ooh, five seconds. Don't try and tell me that the whisky's not mine.'

More laughter.

'Anything more constructive to say before we get out there?' grinned Blizzard when the room had fallen silent again.

'Just give me enough evidence to close the bloody place down,' said the superintendent.

'Couldn't have put it better myself,' said Blizzard and, with a murmuring and scraping of chair legs, the briefing broke up.

Silent and still beneath the emerging moon, the body of George Rawcliffe floated downstream until it drifted gently into the bank, swirled in an eddy and entangled itself among some reeds. For a few moments, it twisted and turned as if engaged in a desperate struggle to free itself from the vegetation's clutches before it gave up the fight and came to a halt. As the moon broke fully through the clouds, Rawcliffe's open eyes stared upwards until, after a few minutes, he tipped over and gently sank beneath the dark waters.

Chapter Eleven

WHEN ROBERT SMART'S mobile phone rang, he was sitting alone and deep in thought in the half light of the lounge at Larch House, cradling a glass of whisky in his hand, occasionally lifting it to let the contents glint in the light from the table lamp. As his phone continued to ring, he glanced over to the grandfather clock: 7.14. He knew who it would be and took the call. At first all he could hear was loud voices in the background, then a man spoke. It sounded like he was on a payphone.

'Robert, it's Henry.'

'Henry, where on earth are you?'

'In a pub. The Red Lion. Seeing some mates.'

'Don't tell me, advising on their stocks and shares?'

'Something like that. Anyway, I'm ringing to say that it's done. The money's on the move.'

'You sure no one knows?' asked Smart.

'What? Plod? No chance. Like I said, they're living in the Dark Ages when it comes to this sort of thing. But they'll catch on one day, Robert, they're bound to. I told you, this had better be the last time.'

'Just keep your nerve, Henry. Do that and we'll be fine.' Smart took a sip of whisky. 'You'll be well enough rewarded, you know that.'

There was a silence at the other end.

'OK, Robert,' said the accountant eventually, 'but I'm warning—'

Smart did not let him finish, replaced the receiver and swilled the whisky in his glass again, a smile playing on his face.

'To my father,' he murmured, raising the glass. 'Long may the bastard rot in Hell.'

When his desk phone rang, John Blizzard was sitting alone in his office at Abbey Road, taking advantage of the pause as officers briefed their teams to compose his thoughts before leaving the station. The inspector glanced at the clock: 7.40.

'Blizzard,' he said, picking up the receiver.

'It's Martin Bartholomew.'

'Isn't it after your bedtime?'

There was silence at the other end.

'Joke,' said Blizzard. 'What can I do you for?'

'The money's on the move. What's more, I know who's moving it. It's definitely Henry Gallen. He got careless this time as well. Makes it easier to track it.'

'Good work,' said Blizzard. After listening for a couple of minutes, he put the phone down, gave a humph of satisfaction and headed for the door, snapping out the light as he walked into the corridor. 'Game on, I think. God, how I love this job sometimes.'

Ten minutes later, the inspector, with Colley in the passenger seat, pulled his Granada into Haverton Street, the row of uniformed officers moving aside to let him edge the vehicle through. A series of police vans with headlights extinguished had already pulled up just down from The Red Lion and the riot teams were assembling quietly and efficiently. As they did so, a man lurched out of the doorway of the pub and spied the gathering. His bleary eyes widened and he turned to run back inside but was too slow; within moments he was being bundled away by a couple of uniformed constables, one of them with a meaty hand across his mouth to silence his cries of warning.

Blizzard pulled his car up behind the vans. He and Colley got out and walked over towards the pub. The inspector saw Katie Summers standing not far away, next to Ramsey. When she noticed him, she smiled slightly. Blizzard nodded.

'Let's hope she's right,' he murmured.

'She's right, no fear on that score,' said the sergeant. 'She's a good 'un, that one. Got her head screwed on the right way. What did she say about coming over here?'

'Asked for time to think about it. Not sure why, I did my best reassuring-boss bit.'

'We'll probably never see her again, then. You didn't do your smile, did you?'

A uniformed officer wearing riot gear approached the inspector.

'Can we go in, sir?' he asked, gesturing to the officers bundling the drunk into the back of the van. 'Don't want to risk anyone else spotting us.'

'Yeah, why not?' Blizzard had already noticed a few curtains twitching in the house. 'Nice and clean, remember.'

'Of course,' grinned the inspector and jogged over to give the command.

Blizzard and Colley stayed on the street as the police teams poured into the building; soon they could hear shouts and the sound of breaking glass and tables being overturned from inside the pub.

'So much for nice and clean,' said Blizzard.

'I'm sure they'll get the Hoover out afterwards,' grinned Colley. 'From what I hear from Katie, there's plenty to choose from. Pick a colour.'

Several men burst through the front door and onto the street, only to be grabbed by waiting officers before they could react. One of them, a scruffy, balding man in a ragged jacket, managed to evade the grasping hands and set off at speed in the direction of the wasteland at the far end of the street, zigzagging drunkenly as he went. Blizzard knew that at the far side of the wasteland was a wire fence and that once over there, he could drop down onto the railway line. Blizzard did not want to risk anything going wrong. The last thing he wanted was a body on the tracks. Not on a night like this.

'Get him back,' he snapped to his sergeant. 'The daft bastard'll get himself killed.'

Colley started to run but Katie Summers was first to react, realizing what was happening and sprinting after the fleeing man. Hearing her footsteps, he turned and glared at her.

'Fuck off!' he hollered. His voice tailed off as he recognized her. 'Ally?'

'You wish.'

'What the...?' he began as he noticed that she was carrying handcuffs.

'Sorry, Clem,' she said with a shrug of the shoulders. 'Duty calls and all that.'

He looked at her in confusion then at Colley jogging up behind her. Recognizing the sergeant, realization finally dawned on his addled brain.

'You're...?' he began.

''Fraid so, Clem.' She produced a warrant card from her jacket pocket. 'Sorry.'

'Bitch,' he snarled and turned to run again.

Summers darted forwards and, within moments, Clem was being marched back up the street, hands cuffed behind his back, muttering drunken profanities as he went. Colley stood by, watching the unfolding scenario with amusement, his assistance not required.

'Pity,' said Summers to the sergeant as they passed him. 'I quite liked him. At least he washes occasionally.'

'Slag!' snapped the man and started to struggle.

'Now, now, Clemmy boy,' said Colley, placing a restraining arm on his shoulder. 'That's no way to speak to the nice lady. In fact, I would rather talk about the outstanding warrant for your arrest instead. Something about unpaid fines, as I recall. Love to know where you've been for the past three weeks. I'm sure the magistrate would like to know as well.'

The comment seemed to calm the prisoner down and he made no protest when he was loaded into one of the vans. Summers stayed to talk to one of the uniformed officers and Colley walked back to his DCI, who had been watching events unfold. As the sergeant approached, the inspector shook his head.

'Too slow, David,' said Blizzard, as they fell into step and headed towards the pub. 'Just too darned slow.'

'Didn't see you running anywhere.'

'Bad back.'

'Of course.' They'd been having the same conversation ever since they started working together.

Reaching the pub, the officers entered the main lounge.

'Ruddy hell,' said Colley, 'what a mess.'

Amid the overturned chairs and tables, a few men were still struggling with the police but most of the drinkers had long since given up the fight and were allowing themselves to be led outside. Nick Towler was behind the bar. He placed a gloved hand on the pump.

'Always fancied doing this,' he said cheerfully. 'Ever since I was a kid. What'll it be, gents?'

'A nicked video or two would do nicely,' said Blizzard.

Towler reached beneath the bar and produced a large cardboard box.

'How about a pint of Knock-Off Special?' he asked, put the box on the bar and fumbled in his jacket pocket, pulling out a piece of paper. Carefully lifting a video machine from the box, he turned it round, squinted as he read the serial number and compared it with the one on the paper. 'Yup, it's one of the those reported after that warehouse was screwed over on Haltby Lane. There's a load more gear in the back office as well. It's jam-packed with the stuff.'

'Katie said it would be.' Blizzard rubbed his hands together. 'Nice result.'

The inspector noticed a gloomy-looking man standing in the passageway behind Towler, trying to shrink into the shadows.

'You the landlord?' asked Blizzard.

The man nodded without enthusiasm; he seemed dazed by the speed and scale of the operation.

'Good,' said the inspector. 'Then perhaps you would care to explain this little lot? Opening a shop, are we?'

Before the landlord could reply, there was a crash behind them as a shaven-headed man squirmed free from an officer's grasp on the far side of the lounge.

'Jackie Gray,' said Colley urgently, as the man started to run across the bar, evaded two more officers, lashing out with a fist and catching one of them in the face, sending him crashing to his knees. 'Wondered when he'd kick off.'

The sergeant gave chase and cornered Gray by the front

door. Gray gave an angry roar and swung a fist but found himself staggering backwards as Colley ducked underneath the blow and delivered an uppercut. Gray's eyes glazed over for a moment then he slumped against the wall, his knees buckling, his face a picture of surprise. A couple of uniforms half-led, half-dragged him outside to the vans.

'Who's too slow now?' beamed Colley, as he walked back to the inspector, rubbing his right hand and wincing with pain. 'It's not just the kids who can mix it, you know.'

Before the inspector could reply, the detectives' attention was distracted by more angry shouting, this time from the snug.

'I've had enough of this,' said Blizzard. 'I really have.'

He strode through to see Baz Garland standing in the corner of the room, eyes flashing with fury as he wielded a broken beer bottle in front of a couple of officers. Tommy Webb and Ron Maskell were already handcuffed and being led towards the door.

'That him?' shouted Garland as Blizzard appeared at the door. 'That the bastard?'

'Wants to see the man in charge,' said one of the officers with a shrug of the shoulders. 'I told him he didn't have an appointment but most insistent, he is.'

'Is he, now?' Blizzard strode up to Garland, who brandished the bottle again.

'Don't come no nearer, pig!' he shouted.

'Oh, cut the crap,' said Blizzard.

The inspected snatched out a hand and twisted the bottle from Garland's grasp, sending it falling onto the carpet. Garland stared stupidly at the inspector for a few moments; it had all happened so quickly. Recovering his wits, he swung a fist but Blizzard swayed out of its way, grasped Garland's wrist and twisted his arm behind him. Garland squealed in pain, uniforms closed in and he felt the cuffs snap on.

'Filth!' he hollered.

'Baz Garland,' said Blizzard, handing him over to a couple of uniforms, 'I am arresting you for still being in the 1970s. Take him away.'

To laughter from several of the officers, Garland was led into the main bar where Katie Summers was picking her way gingerly across the broken glass littering the carpet.

'You!' exclaimed Garland, struggling to get at her but being restrained by one of the uniforms. 'You're a dead woman! A fucking dead woman! Do you hear me? A fucking dead woman!'

Blizzard walked back into the lounge in time to hear the comment. Grim-faced, the inspector strode over and stood close enough to smell the beer on Garland's breath.

'If I ever hear you threaten one of my team again,' hissed the inspector. He left the sentence unfinished and looked at the uniformed officers. ' Get him out of my sight.'

Blizzard noted the troubled expression on Summers' face as Garland was led outside, still uttering threats.

'Don't worry about it,' said the inspector. He tried one of his reassuring looks. 'He's all mouth, that one.'

'I thought we had decided that he wasn't,' she said quietly. 'I thought we had decided that Baz Garland was capable of murder.'

'Yes, but—'

'Sorry, guv,' she said, and walked out of the pub, battling back the tears that threatened to overwhelm her again.

'I really must work on my smile,' said Blizzard, as he and Colley followed her into the night air.

The inspector stood outside the pub for a few moments and watched with approval as the last of the prisoners were loaded into vans. Noticing Arthur Ronald standing further down the street, next to a television crew and a number of press photographers, Blizzard gave a wave. The superintendent waved back; he had a broad smile on his face.

'At least someone's happy,' said Blizzard, and returned his attention to the vans, producing a smile of his own as he recognized one of the young men being bundled into a vehicle. When the man saw the detective, his eyes widened and he tried to duck behind a uniformed officer to avoid being seen but it was too late.

'Well, well,' said Blizzard affably as he walked up to him. 'Henry Gallen, as I live and breathe. What brings a respectable man like you to a place like this, I wonder?'

The accountant smiled weakly.

'Mr Blizzard,' he said. 'What a surprise.'

'The pleasure's all mine,' beamed Blizzard. 'We've got lots of catching up to do, have you and I. Tell you what, why don't we have a chat later tonight? You'll like that.'

Chapter Twelve

'I CAN'T BELIEVE THAT you went to all this trouble just for a few knock-off videos,' said Baz Garland, with a shake of the head. 'There must have been fifty of you fuckers back there.'

'Those knock-off players are worth seven and a half grand,' said Blizzard, glancing at Nick Towler, who was sitting next to him in the interview room at Abbey Road. 'And that's just what we lifted tonight, is it not, Constable?'

'That's right. See, we can trace them back to several jobs carried out in the city in the past six months, and they were worth upwards of seventy grand. Seventy grand, Baz, that's a lot of gear.'

'Yeah, well I don't know nothing about that. Not my style. I keep meself to meself.'

'Actually, I'm not sure that's quite true,' said Blizzard. 'You see, Constable Summers—'

'That bitch!'

'Constable Summers,' repeated Blizzard, 'and I've already warned you about bad-mouthing my officers, seems to think that, rather than keeping yourself to yourself, you are somewhat free and easy with your opinions. Especially about the Smarts, oddly enough.'

Garland looked suspiciously at the inspector.

'This ain't about them videos, then?' he said.

''Fraid not. No, we're much more interested in what you know about Dennis Smart. Much more interested.'

'You ain't got nothing on me,' said Garland quickly. 'I never torched the place. It was kids and you can't prove other—'

'Yeah,' said the inspector, leaning back in his chair, arms behind his head, 'it probably was, but I'm not really interested in that either, to be honest, Baz. Although I can't help feeling that your protestation of innocence fails to convince. However, that's not my main interest.'

Garland looked confused. 'Then what are you—?'

'What really interests me is who murdered Dennis Smart.'

'Murdered?' Garland seemed genuinely surprised. 'I thought the bastard fell down the stairs in that mansion of his?'

'Murdered?' exclaimed Tommy Webb, who was in the neighbouring interview room. 'I thought the bastard fell down the stairs in that mansion of his?'

'I wonder,' said Colley, glancing at the young female detective constable sitting next to him at the table, 'how our Tommy knows that Dennis Smart lived in a mansion?'

'And how do you know he lived in a mansion?' asked Blizzard, leaning over the table and fixing Garland with a hard stare. 'You not been there, by any chance? Don't tell me he invited you to his dinner parties? Somehow, vol-au-vents don't seem your style.'

'Everyone knows they live there,' snorted Garland. 'They creamed off all the cash from the factory to pay for it.'

'That's something we can agree on,' murmured Blizzard, sitting back again. 'But let's stick to the mansion, shall we? You sure you've never been there?'

'Wouldn't be seen dead in it.'

'An unfortunate turn of phrase.'

'Don't try and twist my words. I know what you lot are like. I'm telling you, I don't know nothing about no mansion and I don't know nothing about no murder. I don't care what happens to those bastards.'

'Constable Summers would beg to differ, Baz. She reckons you were making all sorts of threats against them. What's more, she's pretty sure she saw you standing outside the factory last night about the same time as the fire.'

'Ain't no law against standing, is there? And you can't use nothing she says anyway. I know me rights. She's one of them *agent provocateurs*. Besides, I just said those things to impress her.'

'Oh, come off it, Baz,' said Blizzard, feeling suddenly weary as the clock ticked past eleven. 'You've never done anything to impress a woman in your life. We know it's all politics with you. What was it you called the Smarts? Capitalist scum?'

'Yeah, Baz said that,' nodded Webb, 'but it was only words, Sergeant. The beer talking.'

He smiled at the young female constable. She ignored the gesture.

'Keep your mind on the job in hand,' said Colley sharply. 'What about your own view on the Smarts? According to Constable Summers—'

'I still can't believe she's a cop.' Webb shook his head. 'She had us all fooled. Such a nice lass and all.'

'Be that as it may, she did hear you and Garland talking

in aggressive terms about the Smarts on many occasions.'

'Yeah, but I was just trying to impress her.'

Colley looked at Webb's slicked-down hair and shiny black jacket.

'You know,' he said, 'I almost believe you. Maybe it was just Garland killed Smart, then?'

'Baz? He wouldn't murder no one.'

'He's got a fiery temper, though.' Colley ran a finger down a piece of paper lying on the desk. 'A very fiery temper: 1987, convicted of smashing windows at the Jenkinsons factory, '89, assaulted a policeman on a picket line at D L Martins, '91, attacked a worker trying to cross a picket line at Royle Engineering, '93, trashed a director's car at Jacksons, '96....'

'Yeah, but that don't mean he would murder anyone. Look, don't get me wrong, I'm not sad that Dennis Smart is dead, and Baz won't be neither, but he didn't kill him. None of us did.'

'I ain't bothered that he's dead, I admit that,' said Garland. 'Fascist bastard. But I didn't kill him, none of us did, and you ain't got no one can say otherwise, not even your precious Constable Summers.'

'You did threaten to kill *her,* though,' said Blizzard. 'And we've got plenty of witnesses to that. If nothing else, I can charge you for that.'

'Some fucking police officer had my arm twisted behind my back at the time and I was angry. I tell you, it's a police state, that's what—'

'Oh, do give over,' sighed the inspector.

'I want a lawyer.'

'I think you probably do,' said Blizzard, standing up and heading for the door. 'Mind, I can't promise that he's not a fascist bastard. In my experience, most of them are.'

'Funny man,' said Garland.

'Tell me about your father, Tommy,' said Colley, looking down at another piece of paper. 'Alf, is it? Sounds like he's a very ill man.'

Webb's eyes flashed anger.

'Thirty-nine years he worked for them,' he said, animated for the first time in the interview. 'Thirty-nine years and what does he get for it? They wrecked his health and some smart-arse lawyer says we don't get no compensation. We're not greedy people, Sergeant, we only wanted to make some changes to his house so he could stay at home with me mam but they said no. You want to talk about something criminal, Mr Colley, that's criminal.'

'You seem very angry about it.'

'Wouldn't you be?' Webb gave him a look. 'I mean, wouldn't you be? Watching your own father dying like that, bit by bit, day by day, in that shit-hole and no one caring a toss what happens to him? That's what them directors were like. Ripping us off and them in their fancy houses when the rest of us were on the dole. We trusted them and they shafted us. Wouldn't that make you angry?'

Colley surveyed the flushed cheeks and the tears glistening in Webb's eyes.

'I guess it would, Tommy,' he said, 'and maybe I'd want to get my own back on the company an' all. Who knows, maybe I'd even feel angry enough to kill someone for it. Revenge, Tommy, it's a mighty powerful motive in my world.'

'I think I need a lawyer.'

'I think you probably do,' said Colley, standing up and heading for the door.

*

'Trouble is,' said Blizzard. 'They're right, we can't prove anything, can we?'

He looked at the detectives sitting in the CID room as midnight approached; Colley at one of the desks, eating a sandwich, Nick Towler flicking through interview notes, Chris Ramsey with a pile of statements in front of him, Kate Summers drinking from her mug of tea, Graham Ross jotting something down in a notebook, and young Constable Angela Jeffers sitting in reverential silence, fresh from sitting in on the Tommy Webb interview; it was only her second week with the squad and she was feeling a little overawed.

'We've not got a shred of evidence against them,' continued Blizzard, taking a gulp from his mug of tea. 'No forensics, nothing. Maybe they are just a couple of piss-heads shouting their mouths off after all. Someone tell me I'm wrong.'

They all shook their heads.

'What's more,' said Ramsey, holding up a sheaf of papers, 'why them? I was going through the stuff we got when we looked at the factory closure last time. There's plenty others with good reason to hate the Smarts. It's a question of where we start.'

'So what we do?' asked Colley. 'Release them? Just like that?'

Before Blizzard could reply, a uniformed constable walked into the room.

'Sorry to interrupt you,' he said, 'but there's a social worker to see Dave.'

'That'll be for Ron Maskell,' said the sergeant, heading for the door. 'He's pretty impressionable, apparently. Bit of a soft lad.'

'That's all we need,' sighed Blizzard. 'Ask him if he shot JFK while you're at it.'

Colley waved a hand and disappeared into the corridor.

'So what have we got on the Lion?' asked Blizzard, turning to Ramsey.

The detective inspector held up another sheaf of papers.

'Much better news there,' he said. 'Much better. Enough to charge thirteen of them straight off and maybe more when we really get into it. East have offered to take a few bodies because we can't get them all in our cells.'

'They OK with that?' asked Blizzard.

'Got to put them somewhere. Our custody sergeant's tearing his hair out. We're running out of solicitors anyway.'

'That can't be a bad thing,' said Blizzard. He noticed that the uniformed constable was still there. 'Sorry, Bob, was there something else?'

'Yeah, sorry, that accountant you brought in with the others, Henry Gallen? Says he wants to talk to you. Says it's important. I told him you were busy and it would have to wait but he just keeps bang—'

He did not have time to finish the sentence before John Blizzard was out of the office.

'He's keen,' said the constable when he had gone. 'This Gallen guy special?'

'It's a kindergarten thing,' said Ramsey, glancing up at the clock. 'Five minutes twelve seconds. No chance.'

'Tell me, Ron,' asked Colley as he and Maskell sat in one of the stuffy interview rooms. 'Do you know anything about the murder of Dennis Smart?'

Maskell looked away. The sergeant glanced at the young female social worker, who gave a small nod. Colley tried again, his voice gentle, disarming.

'Look, I know this is difficult for you, Ron,' he said. Maskell continued to look away. 'But I really do have to ask. It's really important. Do you know anything about the death of Dennis Smart?'

Maskell shook his head.

'We know you were talking about him with Baz and Tommy,' continued the sergeant. 'At The Red Lion. Are you sure you weren't talking about killing Dennis? If you were, it's in your best interests to tell me.'

Maskell thought. 'They did it,' he said eventually.

Colley sat forward. 'Go on,' he said.

'Baz and Tommy. Baz said he needed a good kicking and that's what he got.' Maskell gave a toothy grin. 'A right good kicking.'

The social worker looked as if she were about to protest, but Colley silenced her with a shake of the head.

'Where was this, Ron?' he asked.

'On the playground near where I live.'

Colley glanced down at Maskell's file. 'The one off Hutton Avenue?' he said. 'With the swings?'

'Yeah, that's it.'

'And when they had finished kicking Dennis Smart? What did they do with the body?'

Maskell thought for a moment then grinned, showing crooked, yellowing teeth.

'We dumped him a rubbish skip,' he giggled. 'He were a real mess, blood everywhere. Baz said his neck was broked. Said he was rubbish so the skip was the best place for him.'

He giggled again. Colley noticed the social worker about to protest.

'Dennis Smart died in hospital,' explained the sergeant

in a low voice. 'After being pushed down the stairs at his home.'

'I told you Tommy was impressionable,' she said.

'I guess so,' sighed Colley, standing up and looking down at Maskell. 'Tell me, Ron, have you ever been to Dallas?'

Chapter Thirteen

'So WHAT DO you want to talk about, Henry?' asked Blizzard, as he ushered a nervous-looking Gallen into the interview room. 'Sit down, please.'

Gallen did as he was told, glanced round the cramped room and felt the almost physical sensation of the walls closing in on him. He eyed the inspector unhappily; he had long since ceased to trust the DCI. After their previous encounter following the closure of the Smarts factory, Henry Gallen had promised himself that he would never return to this room, that he would tell Robert that it was all over, that their arrangement could not be allowed to continue. But Gallen had been weak, he knew that, so here he was, sitting once more in the oppressive silence of the little room and recalling the nightmares that had dragged him from sleep, wide-eyed and shaking, so many times in recent months. Memories of the DCI's steely glares across the desk, the barrage of never-ending questions, the bewildering switches of tactic that left his head spinning, the remorseless ticking of the clock on the wall as day turned to evening turned to night.

Sitting there now, Gallen remembered the rank smell of his own fear as the hours lengthened and recalled the welcome rush of fresh evening air when he was finally released without charge by a visibly irritated chief inspector. Sitting and staring bleakly across at the DCI as he took the seat opposite him at the table, Gallen's mind conjured up once more his feelings of exultation as he had stumbled out of the front door at Abbey Road in February then reminded him how quickly the feeling had been dashed when he turned to see Blizzard standing at the top of the steps, arms crossed as he watched him go. *You'll be back,* the inspector's expression had said. And now he was. Henry Gallen *was* back and he shuddered at the thought.

Blizzard sat and said nothing, a faint smile on his lips as he watched Gallen's turmoil play out on his features. The inspector had long appreciated the value of silence in interviews. As he was fond of telling young detectives, there seemed little sense in doing the work yourself when the suspect's mind could do so much for you. Let it play its tricks, he would say to them. So now Blizzard sat and waited until the sweat began to glisten on Gallen's brow; the inspector loved it when they started to sweat. It was his signal to start the interview.

'Go on then,' he said. 'Spit it out, Henry. What did you drag me down here for?'

'I want to know why I'm being held.' Gallen tried to sound bullish but his voice trembled. 'I have a right to know.'

'Is that all?' Blizzard looked disappointed. 'You're wasting my time, son. The constable said it was something important.'

'Yes, well it is. I've got to meet a client in the morning. It's important that I see him.'

'Allow me to enlighten you, then. Tonight's raid was about the trade in stolen goods going through the Lion. You've probably worked that out for yourself, you're a

112

bright boy. Do you happen to know anything about what's been happening there?'

'No, of course not. I'm a respectable businessman.'

'I'm not entirely sure that a respectable businessman would be found drinking in among the locals at Knock-off Central.'

'I went to school with a few of the lads there, that's all.' Gallen was starting to feel more confident. If Blizzard only wanted to talk about videos.... 'We went different ways after leaving but they're still friends. I've known them for years.'

'Yet you know nothing about the gear they've been passing across the bar?'

'I heard some rumours, I guess, but I'm not involved, if that's what you mean.'

'Actually, I believe you.'

'You do?'

'Hmm. Wrong place, wrong time, Henry. It happens.'

'So can I go if you don't think I've done anything wrong?'

'Everyone's guilty of something, Henry. This client,' said Blizzard casually; he was enjoying himself as he toyed with his prisoner. Time to close the trap. 'The one you're meeting in the morning. Not Robert Smart, by any chance? To discuss a spot of dead man's money-laundering maybe?'

'What?' Gallen tried to conceal his unease. And failed dismally.

'It's a simple enough question,' said Blizzard, giving the slightest of smiles as the sweat glistened ever more brightly on Gallen's forehead.

'Look,' said Gallen, 'we've been through this before, Inspector. I did the company accounts....'

'I prefer the phrase "cooked the books", Henry.'

'I told you last time....'

'I know what you told me,' nodded Blizzard, glancing down at a piece of paper on the desk, letting his gaze linger long enough for Gallen to notice and start to grow anxious about the contents. 'And before tonight maybe I was even prepared to believe that you really were a good, upstanding citizen. I was even going to recommend you to the Rotary Club. And then....' Blizzard tutted and allowed his voice to tail off, appearing to be deep in thought as he ran a finger down a column of figures on the paper. 'And then—'

'And then what?' Gallen looked at the paper. 'What is that?'

'Sorry, Henry, was miles away.' Blizzard gave a smile. 'Like the Smarts' money, oddly enough. We found some of it in Liechtenstein, you know.'

Gallen looked at him in horror; Blizzard could almost hear his confidence shatter.

'Liechtenstein?' said the accountant weakly.

'Yes, it's between Switzerland and Austria,' said Blizzard helpfully. 'I only just found that out today, but I guess you've always known where it is. And guess what? It seems to have got there via you. And, even more remarkably, it went for another walkabout earlier today.'

Gallen had gone white.

'What's more, Henry, we found the money belonging to George Rawcliffe and Jason Heavens as well. Turns out it's also been on holiday.' Blizzard stood up and walked over to stand with his back against the wall. 'You see, Henry, electronic crime is a rapidly developing branch of criminal activity and it is crucial that, as a force, we embrace new forms of less traditional policing in order to ensure that we facilitate its detection.'

Gallen did not reply; he seemed close to tears as the

inspector sat back down at the desk.

'My sergeant did a bit of traditional police work as well,' continued the inspector. 'Still a place for good old shoe leather in the modern police force, and when he checked the security cameras on the newsagent's next to your office, guess who had been in to see you today? Robert Smart, of all people. Can you believe that? And all within hours of discovering that his father was murdered, too.'

'Murdered?' said Gallen quickly. 'I thought it was an accident.'

'Sorry, did I not mention that you're being held as part of a murder inquiry? Apologies, my mistake. Very unprofessional of me. What would my superintendent say?'

Gallen's stare grew bleaker.

'Yes,' continued the inspector. 'Poor old Dennis Smart was murdered and, to answer your earlier question, no, I'm not minded to let you go, not just yet anyway. You see, you are in deep, Henry. Far too deep, if you ask me. The murder changes everything. Lets me push as hard as I want and no amount of complaints to the chief constable can stop me. There's no one to protect you now, sunshine. There's no one to protect any of you.'

'I want a lawyer.'

'I am afraid we're all out of lawyers, Henry. Been a real run on them tonight for some reason.' Blizzard softened his tone. 'Look, son, we'll find you a lawyer if you really want one but hear me out first. You've been a silly boy over this, we can both agree on that, I think, but I'm not after you. I told you that last time, and my offer still stands. Shop the others and I'll see if we can't broker some kind of a deal with the CPS for you. Nothing has changed.'

'Really?'

'Assuming you didn't kill Dennis Smart, no.'

'I didn't!'

'In which case, tell me everything you know, but be warned, Henry, this is the last time I'll make the offer. Turn me down now and I'll throw you to the wolves.'

Which was when Henry Gallen made a decision that was long overdue.

Chapter Fourteen

'ALL OF THEM?' asked Arthur Ronald gloomily, staring across the inspector's desk at a beaming Blizzard early next morning and hoping that he had misheard his friend. And knowing that he hadn't. 'I mean, all of them?'

'The job lot,' nodded the inspector cheerfully. He took a sip from his mug of tea. 'Robert, his tarty wife and that sanctimonious mother of his. And the other two, if we can find them. It's amazing really, they all turned out to be crooks. Who'd have thought it, eh?'

Ronald sighed.

'Look on the bright side,' continued the inspector, thoroughly enjoying himself. 'We don't plan to lift the family gardener.' Blizzard tapped the side of his nose conspiratorially. 'Bridlington, Arthur, Bridlington.'

Ronald closed his eyes, the ramifications playing out again and again in his mind: an irate chief constable, acutely embarrassed because he had been outmanoeuvred by Blizzard and hitting out at anyone and everyone as a result; Blizzard himself triumphant and not minding who knew it; fast-talking lawyers trying to get the Smarts out on bail and protesting their clients' innocence in the media; hungry journalists scenting blood; hordes of.... The superintendent opened his eyes to see Blizzard watching him with a knowing smile on his face.

'You needn't look so bloody smug,' grunted Ronald. 'I take it you are sure about this?'

'The Boy Wonder's taken me through things. We've got them "bang to rights".'

'Are we sure this kid's right?'

'I reckon so. Hardly out of short trousers but red hot on fraud.' Blizzard walked over to the window where he stared down into the police yard, watching a group of officers standing by one of the vans while they smoked their cigarettes. 'You see, Arthur, electronic crime is a rapidly developing branch of criminal activity and it is crucial that, as a force, we embrace new forms of less traditional policing in order to ensure that we facilitate its detection. I am, as you know, very much an adherent of the philosophy that we need to move with the times and that—'

'What on earth are you talking about? You've never moved with the—'

Blizzard guffawed with laughter; it struck Ronald that he had not seen his friend so happy for years. Ronald was not sure he liked it.

'Suffice to say,' grinned the inspector, sitting down at the desk again and reaching for his tea, 'that young Bartholomew can prove that Henry Gallen has been moving cash round for the Smarts directors for years. Quite remarkable what he's done, really. Makes me feel quite old.'

'Everything makes you feel old.'

'Not today,' said Blizzard.

Robert Smart replaced the phone in the living room and turned to face his mother and wife, who were sitting on the sofa.

'According to his secretary,' said Robert, walking over to sit on one of the armchairs, 'Henry Gallen has not arrived for work and he's normally in the office before she is.'

'So maybe he's been delayed,' said Margaret. 'Traffic or something.'

'His secretary reckons he never misses. I told you, Mother, when he rang last night he was in The Red Lion and now it's all over the radio. They've arrested twenty-nine people and you know who was in charge, don't you? John Blizzard, that's who.'

'So? The radio also said it was something to do with stolen DVD recorders. I don't see why you are so worried about it.'

'Because Henry's as weak-willed as they come, Mother. If he *was* arrested last night and Blizzard leans on him, God knows what he'll say. We had all on to keep him quiet last time, remember? He was all for dropping us in it then. I tell you, the little bastard will spill his guts this time. He's terrified of Blizzard.'

'He's right,' said Eleanor, nodding at her mother-in-law.

Margaret considered the comment for a few moments.

'So what do you suggest we do?' she asked eventually. Her tone had changed. Now, she sounded worried.

Robert headed for the door. 'I've already packed a bag.'

'And I'm going with him,' said Eleanor, standing up. 'Can't stay here. Sorry, Margaret.'

Margaret stared at them in amazement. 'But where on earth will you go?' she said.

'Anywhere,' said Robert. 'Anywhere that man can't find us. Do what Heavens did, maybe, go to Spain, live in a big villa with a pool, spend the money. It's not as if we haven't got any, is it?'

'But won't it make us look guilty? Running away?'

'You forget, Mother, we *are* guilty.' Robert turned at the door. 'As sin. Sorry, but I'm not prepared to wait for Blizzard's next visit. He won't stop until he's got us, you know that, and there's no way I intend to spend the next ten years in prison on his account.'

'Yes, but what about your father's funeral?' His mother sounded plaintive. 'You'll miss that.'

'Like I care,' said Robert and walked into the hall.

Eleanor set off after him, hesitated at the door and looked back at her mother-in-law, who sat with her head bowed, her shoulders hunched.

'I really am sorry, Margaret,' said Eleanor. 'I really am but Robert is right. We can't stay here. Not now.'

'But the funeral, love.' Margaret looked at her through eyes glistening with tears. 'I know they never really got on but Dennis *was* his father, surely he cares about that?'

'Do you know,' said Eleanor, walking out of the room, 'I really don't think he does. Not after everything he's done.'

When Eleanor had gone, Margaret sat alone in the living room, her gaze settling on each piece of furniture in turn, as if it were for the last time. The tears finally began to flow as she realized that it probably was.

'So,' said Blizzard, taking a gulp of tea, 'all I need is permission to carry out the arrests before the birds fly the coop, and for you to stand up to the chief should he try to stop me.'

'I take it there are no alternatives?' asked the superintendent, fixing his friend with a look. 'Everyone knows how badly you want the Smarts, John. Are you sure you're not pushing your luck again? It wouldn't be the first time you'd—'

'The evidence is clear and, like I always say, you have to

follow the—'

'Yes, yes, spare me the homilies,' sighed Ronald. 'I take it you reckon that it's all linked to Dennis Smart's murder as well?'

'Ah, well, I'm not so sure about that. They've got their cash already so I can't really see a reason for any of them to kill Dennis. I've gone away from the "falling-out-among-thieves" theory. Best we'll get them on is fraud and the Revenue boys should be able to get some sort of tax evasion charge to stick. That should be enough to see them behind bars for a while. Even the fragrant Margaret.'

'So if they haven't fallen out, why is George Rawcliffe back in the area?'

'That I don't know.' Blizzard frowned. 'And I don't like not knowing things, Arthur.'

Robert Smart leaned against a wall in the hallway, holding his suitcase and staring bleakly at his mother, who was standing defiantly between him and the front door. Eleanor came down the stairs, carrying her bag.

'I'm ready,' she announced.

'Don't try and stop us,' said Robert, as Margaret took a step forward. 'We're going and that's final.'

'I still don't see why we can't just sit tight like we always have. The police did not prove anything last time so why should it be any diff—?'

'For God's sake, Mother,' snapped Robert, finally losing his temper with her, 'I've told you! It's only a matter of time before Blizzard comes back. We didn't just take a few quid, we creamed millions off the company. We took so much the business collapsed; we welched on just about every bill we received in the last six months and we cheated the taxman out of millions. They'll throw the book at us if they find out what we've done. And who knows where it all went, who's the one who can give them chapter and verse? Henry Gallen, that's who. And where's he? In a cell at Abbey Road Police Station, that's where.'

'But what if you're wrong, dear?' Margaret was starting to sound desperate. 'What if Henry doesn't—?'

'I'm not wrong.' Robert pushed past her and opened the front door. 'I'm going.'

'But what about me?' Her voice was quieter now. Plaintive. 'What about me, Robert, who will look after me?'

He looked back at her, his expression softer now.

'Come with us, then,' he said. 'That's your only option.'

'But this is my home.'

Robert shrugged.

'It doesn't feel like mine,' he said.

'So who did kill Dennis Smart, then?' asked Ronald. 'This accountant fellow?'

'Henry Gallen?' snorted Blizzard. 'He may have wanted out but he's a wimp, when all's said and done. Not the type to kill.'

'Ah, yes, but what if he was desperate, John? Pushing Smart down the stairs from behind would be the easiest way to do it. The coward's way.'

'Or the woman's way. Pushing someone from behind does not require much strength.'

'Eleanor, then?' Ronald clicked his fingers. 'Or Margaret. Snapping after years of putting up with her husband's bullying ways?'

'You're clutching at straws, Arthur.'

'Maybe I am but the chief is bound to ask after I've told him that we plan to make him look stupid in front of the whole damned city. It would be nice to have an answer while he's throwing things at me. What about Garland and his mates? They in the frame?'

'Can't see that either. In fact, I've told Chris to release them because we need the cells.'

'I'll take that as a no,' said the superintendent gloomily.

Robert Smart backed the Jaguar out of the double garage and onto the drive, the wheels crunching on the gravel as he did so. He brought the vehicle to a halt and sat in silence for a few moments, arms resting on the steering wheel as he surveyed the house for what he assumed to be the final time. He felt little emotion even though he had lived there since his parents bought it when he was just a kid in shorts. His father had seen to it that Robert had always struggled to summon many happy images of child-hood; there was the odd one of playing on the lawn, of him and the dog running in between the ornamental hedges, images of skinny dips in the pond beyond the greenhouse, all of which should have brought a smile to his face but were instead overshadowed by the looming figure of his father. His bullying, sadistic father who featured in none of the happy memories.

An only child, Robert's relationship with his father had been poor even then, and now, sitting in the car waiting for the women, he scowled at the thought of the beatings and the long hours spent locked in his bedroom for minor transgressions. And he knew that he'd got off lightly; he recalled too many occasions when he sobbed in the dark-ness of his room as his father meted out punishment on his mother downstairs. Robert tried now to blot out the sound of her cries and banished thoughts of his father to the past where they belonged. Robert was glad the bastard was dead. Didn't feel guilty about it. Time to move on.

He honked the horn twice. After a few moments, his mother and Eleanor stepped out of the front door. Margaret turned the key in the lock and paused. Robert sensed that she was crying. He wondered if she would go back in, refuse to leave, but a few moments later both women were in the car, Eleanor in the passenger seat and Margaret in the back, as Robert drove slowly down the drive.

'I suspect we may never return,' he said quietly.

Neither of the women replied.

Unseen as the car passed, the police surveillance officer who had spent a cold and uncomfortable night huddled in among the bushes shrank back into the shadows.

'They're on their way,' he said softly into his radio. 'Best tell your gaffer to get himself over here.'

'No need to look so gloomy, Arthur,' said Blizzard, taking a gulp of tea. 'We've cracked a forty-million-pound fraud and broken up a stolen goods ring all before breakfast. And Chris just took a call from the brewery. They're finally closing the Lion down. The chief should be pleased.'

'Yes, but what do I tell him about the murder? He's bound to ask.'

'Yeah, I know.' Blizzard's gaze strayed to the newspaper cutting still lying on his desk. Something drew his attention once more to the twisted features of the former Smarts supplier Edward Fothergill, and he frowned. 'In most murder cases, you can narrow it down to a suspect pretty quickly but this one just keeps getting bigger. Take this guy,' and the inspector tapped the image of Fothergill. 'Ordinary bloke, mild-mannered, honest as the day is long, and yet look at the expression on his face. In that moment, you could easily believe that he could kill. And he's not alone, Arthur. There must be thirty, forty people in that picture, men, women, and all of them with reason enough to hate Smart and his acolytes. And that's just those who were there. The more I think about it, the less sense it makes.'

'Well, I'll have to tell the chief something about the murder.'

'Ah, but which one?' said Colley, entering the office without knocking.

Ronald looked gloomily at the sergeant.

'Not found Rawcliffe by any chance?' asked Blizzard.

'May well have. Control have just taken a call from a guy who reckons he saw someone being shot down by the river last night. When uniform got there, they found Rawcliffe's car. They reckon it had been there all night.'

'Two down,' said Blizzard, draining his mug and heading for the door.

'Two to go,' said Colley as they walked out into the corridor.

Ronald sighed and picked up the inspector's phone and dialled a number.

'Pam,' he said, 'get me the chief constable, will you? And check when I can claim my pension?'

Outside, Blizzard and Colley were walking down the corridor.

'I keep thinking about Edward Fothergill,' said the inspector, as they approached the stairs. 'Something about the look on his face in that picture, I think. Have you been to see—?'

He did not finish the sentence because his mobile phone crackled into life. He stood and listened to the message for a few moments and slipped the device back into his coat pocket.

'Our Mr Fothergill will have to wait,' he said.

Less than three minutes later, he guided the Granada out of the police yard and into the street where he thrust his foot onto the accelerator, sending the wheels spinning.

It was Robert who first saw the man in the suit standing by the front gate, holding up a hand, instructing him to stop.

'That had better not be one of those poxy journalists,' muttered Robert. 'Because if it is—'

His voice tailed off as he saw the police patrol cars edging into position at the end of the drive, blocking the way into the lane. Several grim-faced uniformed officers alighted and watched him as he edged his vehicle closer. The plainclothes officer who had initially held up his hand stepped forward. Robert sighed and brought the car to a halt a few feet from Nick Towler. The detective constable walked up to the vehicle and gestured for Robert to wind the window down, which he did.

'Why, if it isn't Mr and Mrs Smart,' said Towler, and glanced into the back seat. 'And Margaret as well, by my life. With a suitcase. Going somewhere nice, are we? Going to visit your money? I wouldn't recommend it. DCI Blizzard wants to have a chat.'

Robert cursed and slammed the car into reverse gear, jamming his foot onto the accelerator, startling Towler and sending a shower of gravel flying as the Jaguar careered back up towards the house at high speed, tyres screaming, the vehicle narrowly missing the surveillance officer who was walking down the drive towards him, having emerged from the bushes.

'What are you doing?' cried his mother as the car skidded in front of the house and slewed across the gravel before grinding to a halt. For a few moments, Robert sat with the engine running, his face ashen.

'We can't run, love,' said Eleanor quietly, reaching out to touch his hand as one of the patrol cars appeared on the drive. 'It's over.'

'Maybe it is for you,' said Robert, wrenching open the door, hurling himself from the car. 'I'm not spending the rest of my life in prison!'

'Robert!' shrieked Eleanor, as he started running across the lawn.

She leapt from the car and set out after her husband but by now officers had surrounded the vehicle and she was quickly handcuffed and led away, sobbing bitterly. Towler, his face bleeding where a shard of flying gravel had struck his cheek, held open the rear door of the Jaguar and gestured for Margaret to get out.

'I would not recommend doing anything stupid,' said the constable.

'I can't help feeling that I've done that already,' she said, with a weary smile.

Robert did not look back as he kept running, ploughing between bushes, their branches scratching at his face just like they did in those childhood memories. He could hear the thud of boots behind him and quickened his pace, using his knowledge of the maze of paths to gain him precious time. Soon, he was behind the house, his breathing coming hard as he kept running and the sounds of his pursuers began to fade into the distance. Robert slowed down and leaned against a tree on the edge of the garden, catching his breath until a shout set him off again.

Soon he was at the back wall. Scrambling over it, he dropped onto a ploughed field and started to run again, each step weighed down by cloying mud. More than once, he glanced behind him but no one appeared. Robert had almost reached the far end of the field, and a plan had formed in his mind that if he could just make the next field there was a gate that led onto a small farm track, when there was a shout and, looking back, he saw a couple of uniformed officers appear on top of the garden wall. Glancing to his right, Robert caught a glimpse of the lane through the belt of trees. He had resolved to avoid the road but, noticing that there were now other uniformed officers in the next field, he knew he had no option. He cursed and veered off towards the trees.

Reaching the treeline he scrabbled down a water-filled muddy ditch and plunged through the copse, giving a sigh of relief as he emerged out onto the deserted lane. He began running away from the house but had only gone a few metres when a Granada came slowly round the corner in front of him and pulled to a halt. Robert's heart sank as he saw Blizzard get out of the driver's seat and Colley alight from the passenger's side.

'You're a real piece of work, you are,' said the DCI, walking towards him. 'Leaving the others in the lurch like that.'

Robert turned to flee but saw that the way behind him was now blocked by a patrol car.

'Not sure there's anywhere to run,' said the inspector.

Robert gave an enraged roar and ran hard at Blizzard.

'Get out of my fucking way!' he cried, lashing out a fist at the inspector.

Blizzard swayed inside the blow and snapped out a foot which sent Robert careering to the ground. Before he could regain his senses, his arms had been twisted behind him and handcuffs had been applied.

'Yup,' said Blizzard, dragging him to his feet. 'A real piece of work.'

The inspector glanced at Colley.

'Someone ring the Boy Wonder and tell him there's still a place for traditional policing, will you?' said Blizzard.

Chapter Fifteen

Traditional policing was what took David Colley to Pendower Street shortly before lunchtime. Finding himself temporarily without anything to do, the sergeant recalled his promise to visit Edward Fothergill, whose company had gone bust after the closure of Smarts. Researching the background to the original inquiry, Colley had found that, of all the affected suppliers, Fothergill had been the most vocal. Checking with officers on duty on the day the closure was announced, the sergeant had also discovered that the engineer's anger had taken him perilously close to being arrested as he hurled obscenities at the directors.

Colley parked the car outside number 57 and got out to ring the bell. As he waited for the door to open, he glanced along the tattered terrace, most of the houses characterized by grimy windows and peeling paint. Colley frowned; it was not so long ago that this had been a smart street, literally; standing close to the Smarts factory, the street had been home to many of the workers, families who depended on the factory, who trusted the directors to do right by them. Now, it stood sad and silent, a sign of tough times, a sign of broken promises.

The sergeant's reverie was broken by the undoing of a

lock and the door opened to reveal a small, balding man in his late fifties. He wore a scruffy grey cardigan. The man eyed him suspiciously.

'Whatever you're selling, I don't want it,' he said.

Colley held up his warrant card and, after a few seconds' hesitation, without speaking, Fothergill stood aside to let the sergeant enter the musty hallway then led the way into the gloomy living room, gesturing for his visitor to sit on the sofa.

'I wondered when you'd get round to me,' said Fothergill eventually, as he sat down in an armchair.

'For why?'

'Heard that Dennis Smart was dead. It was on the radio this morning. They said he'd been murdered. I imagine you're checking everyone with reason to hate him.'

'It's purely routine, Mr Fothergill.'

'You can't arrest all of us.' Fothergill gave a slight smile. 'You don't have enough cells.'

'You admit to hating him, then?'

'Hardly an admission.' Fothergill leaned forward in his chair. 'Look, Sergeant, I am glad the bastard is dead. I make no secret of that. Him and the others, they ruined my life. I trusted them and they broke that trust.'

'I heard your business went down because of them,' nodded Colley.

'You don't know the half of it.' Fothergill hesitated and tears started in his eyes. 'My wife....' His voice tailed off.

Colley let him compose himself.

'What about your wife?' he asked eventually, following Fothergill's gaze towards a faded black and white picture on the mantelpiece showing a wedding.

'When the firm closed,' said Fothergill quietly, 'we lost everything. I could not pay any of the lads and the bank

131

said that, if we could not meet our mortgage payments, they would have to repossess the house.'

He looked round the grubby living room.

'It was not always like this,' he said. 'Brenda kept it immaculate. The day after we received the letter from the bank, she had a stroke. Sitting where you are, she was. The consultant said that it could have been brought on by the stress of everything that had been happening. She hung on for a few days before she died....' His voice tailed off. 'Do you know what it's like to watch a loved one die, Sergeant?'

Colley shook his head.

'A little bit of you dies as well,' said Fothergill. 'And you are powerless to stop it happening. So no, I make no secret of my delight that the man is dead. I did not kill him, but, I tell you this, I'll open a bottle of whisky tonight and drink a toast to whoever did. It's not me, though. Never got so much as a speeding ticket.'

'Can you think of anyone else we should speak to?' he asked.

Fothergill gave a mirthless laugh. 'Get yourself a phone book and start at A,' he said. He stood up. 'I am being rude, would you like a cup of tea?'

As he sat in the room listening to the clatter of cups and saucers from the kitchen, Colley found himself staring at the large television standing in the corner of the room. He reached into his jacket pocket for a piece of paper, crumpled because it had been there since the night before. Glancing over towards the door to ensure that Fothergill remained occupied in the kitchen, the sergeant walked over to the television and crouched down behind it, comparing the serial number with the one on the piece of paper. The sergeant shook his head then straightened up as Fothergill re-entered the room carrying the tray.

'Nice television,' said Colley, returning to sit once more on the sofa. 'Where did you get it?'

Fothergill placed the tray on a small side table.

'I can't remember,' he said. It sound evasive.

'I don't think you have to. I think you got it from The Red Lion.'

'That a crime?'

'I imagine the same radio bulletin where you heard that Dennis Smart had been murdered also mentioned that we raided the place last night. I think that you have been handling stolen goods, Mr Fothergill.'

Fothergill sat down heavily on the chair and closed his eyes. The sergeant let him compose his thoughts.

'I was desperate,' said Fothergill eventually. 'My old telly was knackered and one of the lads at the Lion offered me that one.' He gave a slight smile. 'It's a Countdown thing. Am I under arrest?'

'Well, if I was to—' began the sergeant but did not have the chance to finish the sentence because his mobile rang.

The sergeant took the call in the hallway then walked back into the living room where Fothergill eyed him anxiously.

'*Am* I under arrest?' he repeated.

'Not at the moment,' said the sergeant. 'Like you said, we wouldn't have enough cells. Out of interest, how much did it cost you?'

'Twenty quid.'

Colley walked out into the hallway, shaking his head.

'I'm in the wrong game,' he said.

'You speak as if I have committed some kind of transgression, Chief Inspector,' said the heavily bearded man sitting behind his cluttered desk and eying the detective keenly.

'Maybe you have, Professor,' said Blizzard. 'I doubt that Henry Gallen could have done what he has done without your assistance.'

'A somewhat unfair comment.'

The two men were sitting on the eleventh floor of the sixties concrete tower block which loomed over the University of Hafton. A long-time admirer of good architecture, Blizzard had always disliked the block and his distaste for the university had not been helped by the Out of Order sign on the lift doors that morning, forcing him to climb the stairs. His mood had not been improved by the sight of Roy Meehan's scruffy little office, with piles of books, papers and empty pizza boxes covering most of the floor. The professor himself had done little to endear himself to the inspector; in his mid-thirties, he was scruffily dressed, his hair was unkempt and crumbs flecked his beard.

'I'm not so sure it's unfair,' said Blizzard. 'So tell me, why *did* Henry Gallen come to your school of crime?'

'I hardly think that education can be described as a crime, Chief Inspector. That tends to be the type of philosophy adapted by totalitarian states. Besides, Henry's an accountant, a perfectly legal occupation. Not even your somewhat one-dimensional view of the world can dispute that.'

'Well, your student seems to have taken a somewhat liberal view of his oath,' grunted Blizzard. 'What was the course that he took?'

'Electronic Crime in a Post-Capitalist Age.'

'And what the hell is that when it's at home?'

'It's an evening class that runs over twelve months. Very popular.'

'I'll bet it is.'

'It's all above board,' said the professor. 'They get a diploma at the end of it. And it's sponsored by Eastern Counties Bank.'

'Do they know that you have been telling your students how to siphon money out of other people's accounts?'

'Another unfair comment, Chief Inspector,' said Meehan calmly. 'Besides, I prefer to say that I tell them how other people siphon money off. Oh, no need to look so disapproving. Just a little jokette. In fact, you should be sending some your officers along. In my view, the police are way behind when it comes to the investigation of electronic crime. You see, electronic crime is a rapidly developing branch of criminal activity and—'

'Yes, spare me the lecture,' said Blizzard. 'I've already had it from one of your protégés.'

'I assume you mean Martin Bartholomew?'

Blizzard nodded. 'He seems to take the view that I am some sort of dinosaur.'

'A bright young man, is Martin,' said Meehan, allowing himself a slight smile when the detective scowled at him. 'Very perceptive indeed. You could learn a lot from him. Picks things up very quickly.'

'And Henry Gallen?' asked Blizzard sourly. 'Did he "pick things up" quickly?'

'Quickly enough.'

'Quickly enough to be capable of moving money from country to country without anyone knowing?'

'Without the police knowing, maybe. Not that that would be difficult. Oh, there's the look again. I know what you are thinking, Inspector, but the university is a seat of learning and we cannot be held responsible for what our students do with what we teach them. I mean, our History

Department runs a course on the rise of the Nazi Party in the 1930s, that does not mean we expect our students to invade Poland.'

'Yes, but is it really wise to—?'

'Look, the course was designed to raise awareness of the problem. I see nothing wrong in that. Unless, of course, you are one of those individuals with closed minds who sees no value in education. In which case, young Martin was correct, you are a dinosaur.'

A glowering Blizzard was about to reply when his mobile rang.

Chapter Sixteen

'SORRY,' SAID BLIZZARD, staring across the Haft's murky waters before glancing at Colley, who was standing next to him on the path, 'remind me why I'm standing here freezing my butt off when Robert Smart's sitting in a nice warm cell at Abbey Road?'

'You'll see,' replied the sergeant enigmatically, tapping the side of his nose. 'Little party trick.'

Blizzard glanced upstream, only just able to make out in the distance the police officers searching the trees ranged along the river, their figures barely visible in the gathering early-afternoon mist.

'And how come we're nowhere near where the shooting is supposed to have happened anyway?' he asked grumpily. 'Surely they're in the right place and we're in the wrong one?'

'All in good time.'

'Why was the witness there anyway?' asked Blizzard, peering into the mist to better make out the searchers. 'And how come he didn't report it when it happened like any normal human being would?'

'I told you, he had been making out with a hooker in the trees when he heard voices then a splash. Looked out, presumably having pulled his trousers up first, and saw what he thought was a body in the water and someone walking away with a gun in their hand. Last thing he wanted was to confront someone with a gun and he was even more frightened of what his missus would say if she found out what he'd been doing. This morning, he had an attack of conscience and called us. The Lord does indeed move in mysterious ways.'

'What?'

'He's a vicar,' grinned Colley. 'The Baptist place at the top of Keeble Avenue. The one who keeps writing letters to the paper complaining about declining morals. I imagine he's doing research for Sunday's sermon.'

The revelation appeared to cheer Blizzard up, but it was only a brief respite and he soon returned to his gloomy perusal of the riverbank.

'But we're still no nearer to finding where the body is,' he said.

''Fraid not. The Lord's not being that accommodating. We've got officers searching all along the bank.' The sergeant gestured downstream this time, towards another group of uniformed officers struggling through the tangled vegetation clogging up the shallows. 'It's a bit of a needle-in-a-haystack job, though. He could be anywhere.'

Blizzard nodded gloomily; he knew the reedbeds well, had spent many happy hours walking along this stretch of the river, thinking, allowing his mind to settle during difficult inquiries. The inspector had always responded well to the soothing effect of lapping water and, as a scholar of industrial history, loved to pick his way alongside the remnants of factories and warehouses lining the Haft. He'd often toyed with the idea of writing a book on the decline of the area's industry but somehow it never seemed to happen. However, as the mist continued to close in, damp and cloying, even he struggled to identify particular spots among the featureless expanse of vegetation.

Blizzard sighed and turned up his coat collar; the river was doing little for his state of mind on this occasion.

'How long have they been looking?' he asked.

'Best part of an hour. Some stretches are too deep so the inspector called in the divers but they're tied up on a job over at Bradby and won't be here until later. They've been searching a quarry for that old boy who went missing.'

'This could be a long day,' sighed Blizzard. 'I forgot to ask, how did it go with Fothergill?'

'Blames the company for his life falling apart but I can't see him being the murderer. We could get him for handling, mind, nice telly in the living room. You get to see Professor Meehan?'

'Accused me of being a dinosaur.'

'Surely not. Ah, here we go,' said the sergeant as a guttural, throbbing sound invaded the thick silence. 'We called in the police launch and, when he heard what was happening, their skipper asked us to meet him here.'

'Why?'

'You'll see.' Colley watched the shape appear round a bend in the river, indistinct at first but gradually taking the form of a somewhat battered boat. 'Just hope his little trick works. Save a lot of time.'

'I wouldn't get too hopeful.' Blizzard gestured to a section of the river where the water swirled and eddied. 'Get caught up in that little lot and Rawcliffe would be at the sea and halfway to Holland in no time.'

'The skipper reckons not. He seemed pretty sure that Rawcliffe is nearer than we might think.'

'That's assuming it is Rawcliffe. You check how many other missing people we have?'

'Too many. Thirty-two city-wide. Nine of them in Western, including that woman who vanished while walking her dog last month. But not all of them left their car on the bank.'

'Good point.' They stood for a few moments, watching as the boat edged its way across the river. 'Fee OK last night? You weren't back till well after two.'

'She was asleep. I tried not to make any sound as I came out this morning but she woke up. I made her a cup of coffee.'

'You and your coffee.'

Blizzard gave a rueful smile. 'What else can I do, David? I know sod all about kids and even less about pregnant women, except that they're unhinged most of the time.'

'You're doing fine.'

Blizzard sought humour in the sergeant's expression but found nothing. In his quieter moments, the inspector worried that familiarity was breeding disrespect in the sergeant. They'd worked together for several years and Blizzard had grown to trust him even more than Ronald, yet recent weeks had seen a string of comments which suggested that the line between employer and employee had become blurred by friendship; his concerns had not been helped by the sweepstake. For all their friendship, the fact remained that Blizzard was still Colley's senior officer and demanded respect. Such thoughts worried the inspector because he was not sure of the question, let alone the answer.

'What's wrong?' asked the sergeant, noticing his boss surveying him.

'Nothing,' said Blizzard, reaching out and touching the sergeant lightly on the arm. He sensed he already had his answer. 'Thanks for the reassurance. It's much appreciated. Always is.'

'Least I could do,' said Colley, smiling slightly. 'And I always like to do the least.'

'You need a new scriptwriter.'

'You could be right,' chuckled Colley, noticing that the launch had edged as close to the reeds as it could. 'Time to engage with Captain Bird's Eye, I think.'

Blizzard raised an eyebrow.

'Laura's into fish fingers,' explained the sergeant. 'She'd have them for breakfast, lunch and tea if she could. You've got all this to come. And you need to make sure you're up to speed on the Munch Bunch before the babby arrives.'

A uniformed inspector appeared on the boat's deck and waved cheerily across to the detectives.

'If this works I'll look like a genius,' he bellowed. 'If it doesn't, I'll look like a right dickhead.'

'There's reassuring,' murmured Blizzard.

'These nautical coves, eh?' grinned Colley.

Several other officers appeared on deck and peered across at the reeds. One of them dipped back into the cabin and reappeared with a pair of binoculars with which he scanned the river. He pointed further downstream, the officers had a discussion and the boat moved off fifty metres before heading in towards the side once more where the crew perused the bank again. They repeated the exercise several times until the boat was more than a quarter of a mile away from the detectives, at which point it spun round slowly until its stern was pointing towards the bank. The pilot gunned the engine and the water foamed and thrashed as the launch worked its way slowly along the fringes of the reeds, throwing up clouds of silt and dying vegetation and risking entanglement. A shout went up and a large shape floated out into open water to be hooked and hauled on board by the crew.

'Well, I'll be ...' murmured Blizzard, as the launch headed downstream to a nearby jetty. He stared at the sergeant in amazement. 'That's one of the most remarkable things I've ever seen. How on earth did he know it was there, then?'

'Reckons he's done it before. Fished some old geezer out ten years ago. He wittered on about water flows and the like but I had no idea what he was banging on about. I guess it would have helped if I was listening.'

Blizzard and Colley headed back to the inspector's Granada and, after a short drive, were soon walking along the crumbling jetty, which had been once used by a fruit merchant before his warehouse fell victim to recession in the eighties. The skeletal remains of the building stood nearby, bearing the scars of numerous vandalism attacks, its windows long since smashed and its walls plastered with vulgar graffiti. The jetty served nothing but waste-land littered with the rotted remnants of pallets.

The launch had already tied up and a knot of police officers had gathered round the body, which the crew had carried ashore and placed gently on the slipway. They parted to let the detectives through.

'How's that for a trick?' shouted the skipper, who was still on the launch with a coil of rope in his hand. 'Good enough for you?'

'Very impressive,' said Blizzard. 'You should get yourself booked for bar mitzvahs.'

As the others laughed, the inspector looked down at the bloated features. They were still recognizable.

'Reckon that's him?' asked one of the marine officers. 'That your man, sir?'

'Yeah,' said Blizzard grimly. 'It's George Rawcliffe all right.'

Colley crouched down and carefully pulled back the sodden overcoat. Finding no sign of an injury on the front of the body, he turned the corpse over to reveal a neat bullet hole in Rawcliffe's shirt.

'Victim,' said the sergeant, looking up at Blizzard. 'Definitely a victim.'

'Good heavens,' said the inspector.

Back at Abbey Road, Robert Smart kept banging on the cell door until the custody sergeant arrived and slid open the grille to see the prisoner standing up close and glaring at him.

'What do you want?' asked the sergeant curtly. 'I've got enough to do without worrying about you.'

'How long will I be here?'

'Until the DCI gets back.'

'How long will that be?'

'I don't know. He's been called out on a job.'

'And where's my lawyer? And where's my wife? And my mother?' Smart glared at him. 'I know my rights. We've been here for hours and—'

'Hush your mouth,' said the sergeant curtly, turning away. 'They're fine, which is more than they deserve.'

'What did you say?' Smart walked up to the grille. 'Go on, what did you say?'

'I said it was more than they deserve,' replied the sergeant, turning back. 'More than any of you deserve, if you ask me.'

'And what exactly do you mean by that?' demanded Smart.

The sergeant walked over to peer through the grille until their faces were a matter of inches apart.

'You're the lowest of the low,' he said, his voice low and

hard. 'You all are. Fucking scum.'

'Now, hang on—'

'My father was laid off when you closed the factory,' said the sergeant, voice trembling with emotion. 'Thirty-six years he'd been with you. Hasn't worked since. No one's employing men like him these days. You wrecked his life, absolutely wrecked it. Fit as a lop, he was, and do you know what happened last week? Do you? He had a heart attack, that's what. Lucky to be alive, the doctors say.'

'Yes, but you can hardly bl—'

'And now I hear that you were creaming money off after all,' snarled the sergeant. 'Money that could have kept my dad and others like him in work. You're a fucking disgrace, son, and I hope Blizzard throws the bloody book at you. There's plenty more in this police station feel the same as me, folks as knew people who worked there, so if you know what's good for you, you'll stop the whining and keep your trap shut.'

With that, the custody sergeant stalked back down the corridor, leaving Robert Smart feeling alone and frightened as the walls of his cell closed in on him.

Katie Summers was walking up the drive towards Abbey Road Police Station when the main door swung open to reveal Baz Garland, Tommy Webb and Ron Maskell, unkempt and unshaven after their night in the cells. The constable contemplated turning back but it was too late; they had already seen her from their vantage point at the top of the steps.

'Well, well, well,' sneered Garland, walking down towards her and standing so close that she could smell his stale breath, 'if it isn't Constable Scumbag.'

Summers made as if to brush past him but the others

blocked her way and Garland grasped her arm, making her cry out in pain.

'You're a dead woman,' rasped Garland. 'I promise you, a dead woman.'

'Get off!' She wrenched herself free.

'You can run all you like but we won't forget this,' shouted Garland as she stumbled up the steps, tears half-blinding her. 'Your pal Blizzard can't protect you all the time. We'll find you, you bitch, and we'll do for you.'

He and his friends continued down the drive, their mocking laughter ringing in the constable's ears as she stood trembling at the top of the steps and found herself overwhelmed by tears once again.

Chapter Seventeen

'I HAVE JUST BEEN talking to a friend of yours,' said Blizzard, looking across the interview room table at the unkempt and hunched figure of Henry Gallen and ignoring his solicitor. 'One Professor Meehan.'

Gallen viewed the inspector with a look of resignation through bloodshot eyes; it was early afternoon and he had been at the police station for sixteen hours with no sign of the ordeal coming to an end.

'Not surprisingly,' continued the inspector, 'he confirmed what you said. Turned you into a right international criminal, didn't he?'

'He didn't mean to.'

'Maybe so but I can't help thinking that he told you much more than was perhaps wise in the circumstances.'

'He had no idea what I was up to. Just thought I was keen to learn.'

'Maybe he should have thought a bit more about what he was doing, then,' said Blizzard. 'Presumably when you walked into his classroom for the first time, you did not know much about electronic crime yet when you finished the course there you were, remarkably skilled in fraud. Even had a diploma in it to stick on the wall. If your beloved professor had been running seminars on how to

146

commit burglary, we'd be charging him with acting as an accessory.'

'Your views on the education system are all very interesting, Chief Inspector,' said the lawyer, a humourless, thin man in a dark suit, 'but perhaps we can get to the matter in hand. What is going to happen to my client?'

'We will have to charge him, of course.'

'Even after all the assistance he has given you?'

'I can't ignore what he's done, Mr Stevens,' said Blizzard. 'However, his help will, I am sure, be seen as a mitigating factor. If he can convince the judge that he did it under duress from Robert Smart, he might even get away with a suspended sentence.'

Gallen looked at him hopefully. 'Can I go when you have charged me?' he asked.

'As long as you don't skip town. The last thing we want is you going walkabout like the money.'

Thirty minutes later, John Blizzard was sitting in his office, gratefully sipping a mug of tea which he cradled in hands which still felt cold even though he'd been back from the riverbank for the best part of an hour. There came a light knock on the door and, looking up, he saw Summers standing there; she appeared to have been crying.

'What's wrong?' he asked, gesturing for her to come in.

'I want to go back to Lincolnshire,' she said, sitting down. 'I want to go back now.'

'Why the rush?' said the inspector. He decided not to try a reassuring smile; he'd learned his lesson. 'Has something happened?'

'I bumped into Baz Garland,' she said, starting to cry again. 'On his way out of the station a few minutes ago. He threatened me again. Said I was a dead woman.'

'Yeah, but I told you he's all gob, that one. Now some of

our real bad....'

His voice tailed off as her tears came faster; Blizzard was not quite sure what to say. He had always struggled with tears; he had never coped well when Fee turned on the waterworks, which had happened more and more as the birth approached. The inspector wished Colley was in the office now; Colley would know what to say. He had the gift, the right word at the right time. The inspector handed Summers a handkerchief, noting with embarrassment that it was somewhat grubby, but it seemed the only thing he could do and she did not seem to notice its condition.

'Don't worry, Katie,' he said, attempting to sound reassuring. 'Baz Garland won't hurt you, I'll see to that.'

'Maybe he won't hurt me,' she said, dabbing her eyes with the handkerchief, 'but I'm sorry, I really don't think I'm cut out for being a detective in Hafton.'

'What, just because some gobshite has a pop?' Blizzard noticed the sudden look of defiance on her face and held his hands up. There was little point in arguing and he was already regretting the insensitive way his comment must have sounded. 'OK, if you're sure. You know where we are if you change your mind, though.'

She nodded.

'But don't rush it,' he continued. 'You've been through a lot this past month. Maybe you'll feel different in a day or so.' He decided to take a leaf out of Colley's book and try humour. 'Once you've arrested a couple of sheep, you might think differently.'

To his relief, she managed a weak smile.

'Look,' he said. 'You've the makings of a good cop, a very good cop, and I really could use someone like you around here. So give it a few days, eh?'

'My mind really is made up. I really *am* sorry.'

She stood up, handed back the soggy handkerchief and walked out of the office. Once she had gone, Blizzard sat and thought for a few moments then smiled as a thought struck him.

'As one door closes,' he murmured, snatched up the phone and dialled Ramsey's number.

'Chris,' he said, 'I know you're busy but I want our friend Baz Garland brought back in.'

'But I've just let him go,' protested the detective inspector. 'Like you told me to. You said there was not enough evidence to hold him and, if you recall—'

'I know what I said, Chris, but I will not have him threatening my officers. I shouldn't have let the little shit get away with it the first time.'

Ramsey was about to reply when he looked out of his office and saw a tearful Katie Summers walk along the corridor, being comforted by Constable Jeffers. The detective inspector scowled and his tone changed.

'Don't worry,' he said into the phone. 'I'll get someone to lift him straight away. Garland's feet won't touch the ground.'

'Good man. Oh, and tell Versace that I want Garland's house searched again. See if we missed anything.'

'What we looking for, though? Ross reckons there's nothing to link him to the murders.'

'So get him looking for anything that connects him to the fires at Smarts. Even if he didn't kill anyone, maybe we can get him for that. I'm not going to let the bastard wriggle out of this. Everyone is guilty of something.'

'Right you are.'

As the chief inspector replaced the receiver, a uniformed sergeant popped his head round the office door.

'Can you ring your missus, John?' he said. 'She's rung a

couple of times.'

'She's not—?' began Blizzard, realizing with a stab of guilt that Fee had been pushed to the back of his mind.

'Na, nothing like that, think she just wanted a chat.'

'OK. Thanks, Charlie.' Blizzard dialled the number.

Fee answered straight away.

'Sorry I missed your calls,' said Blizzard. 'Been a bit busy here. You OK?'

'Just taking it easy, really. Feeling a bit tired.'

'I know how you feel.'

'I very much doubt it, John.'

Blizzard frowned; it was so easy to say the wrong thing, he thought.

'Sorry, love,' she said before he could reply. 'Uncalled for. Just want this all to be over. I'm going up the wall here, sick of waiting. Never thought I'd ever say that I missed the villains of Hafton but I do. How's the inquiry going?'

'Not sure, really. Everything else is just about wrapped up but I've still no idea who killed our two guys, or if they were even done by the same person for that matter. Different MO. Rawcliffe was shot in the back.'

'Ah, but they're not different MOs, are they?'

'Meaning?'

'Well, Dennis Smart was pushed down the stairs from behind and now this Rawcliffe fellow gets shot from behind as well. Like Arthur said, it's the coward's way, isn't it? Whoever did it can't bring themselves to face their victims. If you ask me, you're looking for a Yellowbelly.'

'You leave the good folk of Lincolnshire out of this.'

'You know what I mean, John. Maybe the factory is not the link after all. Maybe what you're looking for is someone who's not strong enough to kill them face-to-face.

A woman maybe?'

'Yeah, we had considered that. Trouble is we've got nothing definite linking anyone to the killings. I dunno, love, everywhere you turn you run into a brick wall.'

'Sounds like you'll be late tonight, then.'

'I fear so.'

'Try not to be too late, then. I need a cuddle.'

'A cuddle sounds nice,' said Blizzard, as Colley walked in. The sergeant turned to leave but the inspector gestured for him to stay. 'Got to go, love. Talk later.'

'Chief Constable?' asked Colley, sitting down at the desk. 'Glad to see you and him getting on better.'

'Yes, thank you, Sergeant,' said Blizzard with a smile; he was already regretting the way he had doubted Colley earlier in the day. The inspector had long appreciated his colleague's ability to inject humour into situations. 'Any news?'

'The air is full of alibis. Oh, and Robert Smart's kicking off alarming. Custody sergeant says he keeps demanding to see you. Banging on about his rights.'

'He in the mood to confess?'

'Not from what the sarge said.'

'Then he's not got any rights.'

'An interesting interpretation of PACE, if I may say so.'

'It'll do him good to sweat on it for a while,' said Blizzard. 'How are the women?'

'Margaret's pretty upset, I think. Pretty sure she's never been in a police cell before. The custody sergeant reckons Eleanor's more sanguine about it. She used to work for the Met, apparently. Gives the impression she knows her way round the system.'

'I take it none of them knows that we've released Henry Gallen?'

'Not as far as I know.'

'Keep it that way. I want to keep the pressure up. Oh, I've asked the DI to lift Baz Garland again.'

'Yeah, I heard. Katie was in bits about it.' Colley pursed his lips. 'I was surprised, to be honest. Thought she was tougher than that.'

'So did I. Garland has probably lost me a damned good officer and I'm not in the mood to let the little toerag get away with it.'

'Shouldn't prove too problematic to track him down this time of day,' said Colley, glancing at his watch. 'He'll not have gone far. Just a question of finding out where they're going to drink now that we've closed the Lion down.'

Just after 3.30, with the afternoon mist starting to shroud the small railway station a short walk from The Red Lion, Katie Summers placed her suitcase on the largely deserted platform and sat down on one of the benches. It felt damp and cold. Nervously, she looked both ways, anxiously seeking out familiar faces, anyone who might know her from the pub. Anyone who might spell danger, who might alert Garland.

Her reaction to the earlier encounter had surprised her; she, too, had assumed she was made of sterner stuff. She'd faced down plenty of criminals back in Lincolnshire, lads nastier than Garland, farm lads, handy with their fists, tough as nails, prepared to use a weapon if there was one to hand, but something about the look on Baz Garland's face had unsettled her. Perhaps, she thought, as she continued her perusal of the platform, it was his eyes, the wild look in those eyes of his. She could not remember having seen anything quite like it, except in the newspaper cutting that the DCI had left on his desk. She'd seen that same twisted look of hatred there as well and, having seen it for herself now, she was prepared to believe that Garland was capable of anything.

She shuddered at the thought and continued her perusal of the platform. To her relief, she did not see anyone she recognized, a couple of business travellers in smart suits, both more interested in their newspapers, and a mother struggling to control three lively young children, two of whom were pulling each other's hair. All very innocent, but the sick feeling in the pit of Katie Summers' stomach confirmed to her that she was right to leave Hafton and head back home to Lincolnshire.

As the late-afternoon light started to fade, Baz Garland emerged from a run-down terraced house in the next street down from The Red Lion, clutching a brown paper parcel.

'Thanks, mate,' he said.

'Whatever you're going to do, don't tell anyone where you got it,' said the scruffy man in the doorway. 'And wipe the prints off it after you've used it.'

Garland waved a hand of acknowledgment and, after the door slammed, took a furtive look up and down the street before cutting through a back alley to come out almost opposite the Lion, which now stood boarded up, with the notice of closure pinned to the door and a bored-looking uniformed officer standing guard outside the front door. Garland cursed; he had not expected the police to still be there, and he quickly ducked back into the alleyway. He walked quickly back into the other street, shaking his head and muttering to himself. Damned-fool mistake, he thought angrily. The last thing he wanted was to be confronted before he had the chance to finish the job; which was when he saw the police car emerge from the main road and noticed the uniform in the passenger seat point him out to the driver.

'Shit!' exclaimed Garland, who turned and started to run down the street, acutely conscious that the patrol car was closing in on him all the time.

Breathing coming hard and fast, he reached the wire fence alongside the railway line. For a few moments, he considered trying to climb it, planning to escape across the tracks, but that would mean jettisoning the parcel and he could not afford to do that. He was in enough trouble as it was. With a muttered curse, he turned to face his pursuers, fixing them with a baleful look. The police car drew to a halt and the two officers got out.

'The DCI wants a little chat with you, Baz,' said one of them, approaching him.

'I just been released.' Garland tried to keep his voice calm. 'Your lot let me go. They know I ain't done nothing wrong.'

'Yeah, well, the DCI has changed his mind and he wants you back in. Reckons you've been picking on innocent young girlies. You get your kicks doing that, Baz?'

'She deserved it.'

'Not sure the DCI sees it that way,' said the officer, closing in on him.

'Stay back!' shouted Garland.

'Oh, come on, sunshine,' said the constable, 'don't make this any harder than it has to be. There's nowhere for you to run.'

Instinctively, Garland hugged the parcel close to him.

'What's that?' asked the other uniform, noticing the gesture.

'None of your business.'

'It's all my business, Baz.' The officer took a step

forward. 'Come on, let me see it.'

Garland backed up against the fence, hands feeling for the reassuring shape of the gun through the brown paper.

Chapter Eighteen

'How will what happened at The Red Lion last night affect your crime figures, Chief Inspector?' asked one of the reporters. 'Last month's stats were up, weren't they? You must be a happy man.'

From his vantage point behind a desk at the front of the Abbey Road briefing room, John Blizzard looked out at the gathered journalists without much enthusiasm. Two television cameras were filming him and a couple of radio reporters were recording his comments; there was also a smattering of newspaper reporters, one of whom had asked the question.

Blizzard had always detested dealing with journalists but he had also long realized that, if you wanted to get a message out, then the media was the only way to do it and the raid on the pub and the revelation about the murder of Dennis Smart – the force had not yet released any detail on Rawcliffe's death – had excited plenty of media interest. Before he replied to the reporter's question, the DCI glanced over to the back of the room where Chris Ramsey and Colley were leaning against the wall, standing next to Arthur Ronald, who had a slightly anxious look on his face, born out of previous experience of his friend's fractious relationship with the media. The phrasing of the question had not done much to ease his concerns.

'Actually,' said Blizzard to the journalist who had asked the question, 'it was the first time the crime stats had been up for nearly four years. Besides, do you not think that on this occasion, a little bit of credit for the police would be in order? The Red Lion has long been a thorn in the side of this force and the news that it has been closed down by the brewery will delight a great many people. It's last orders for a lot of criminals.'

He'd been working on his soundbites. Ronald nodded approvingly.

'Last night's raid,' continued Blizzard, 'led to us seizing a significant amount of stolen property and seventeen people have been charged to date with more to come. It sends out a message to our criminal fraternity that we will not tolerate their activities. So, yes, I'm a happy man and me being happy is a rare thing indeed, as some of you well know.'

A number of journalists laughed; few of the reporters could remember seeing him happy. Blizzard glanced round the room, noting a number of journalists with whom he had clashed in the past, and caught Ronald's eye. The superintendent could not recall when last he had heard laughter at a John Blizzard press conference. If ever. Perhaps, he thought, irritated chief constable or not, it would be all right, after all.

The station announcer's voice came over the crackling tannoy.

'The next train arriving at Platform 2 will be the 15.09 to Lincoln,' he said. 'This train is running three minutes late.'

'Can't come soon enough,' muttered Katie Summers and

glanced at her watch; soon she would be out of Hafton for good. She had no intention of returning.

'Now come on, son,' said one of the uniforms, holding out a hand to Baz Garland. 'Show us what's in the parcel.'

'Believe me, you don't want to see what it is.'

'Stop playing games, Baz,' said the officer and both he and his colleague stepped forward. 'Show us what's in the parcel.'

'You asked for it,' said Garland, feeling strangely light-headed as he unwrapped the parcel to reveal a revolver.

'Can I ask about the murder of Dennis Smart?' asked a reporter a few minutes into the press conference. 'Can you tell us how he died? We all thought he slipped and fell down the stairs.'

'Join the club.'

'Does that mean you got it wrong?'

Ronald closed his eyes; past experience had taught him that such questions evoked volatile reactions from Blizzard. On this occasion, however, the chief inspector kept calm and shook his head.

'Nobody got anything wrong,' he said. 'Fresh information came to light, that's all.'

'Has anyone been arrested yet?'

'Not yet,' said Blizzard, choosing his words carefully, 'although I can confirm that we are talking to several people of interest. This is, as I am sure you are aware, ladies and gentlemen, part of a long-running and extremely complex inquiry.'

'So is the murder definitely linked to the rumours that there was a large-scale fraud connected to the closure of the factory, then?'

'All I am saying, Malcolm, is that the events surrounding the closure of Smarts may be of some relevance.'

'So was Dennis Smart killed because he stole the money?'

'When did you ever know me to speculate?' said the inspector. 'Good job I'm in a good mood.'

'But everyone knows that you believe the directors were on the take,' persisted the radio reporter. 'You've not exactly made a secret of your views so why not just come out and say it?'

'No comment.'

'Come on, Inspector.'

'No comment.'

'You can't go all coy on us now,' said another journalist.

Arthur Ronald held his breath; Colley glanced at Ramsey and wondered what would come next. Ramsey, for his part, shrugged. John Blizzard smiled again.

'Been called many things, Brian,' he said, 'but never coy.'

One or two of the reporters laughed and Arthur Ronald gave an audible sigh of relief.

Baz Garland levelled the revolver at the officers, both of whom took several steps back.

'Come on, son,' said one of them, noticing with alarm that Garland's hand was steady but that there was a wild look in his eyes. 'Hand it over.'

'Get back,' said Garland, taking a step forward. 'Or so help me, I'll shoot. I'll blow you away.'

'One more thing,' said another journalist as Blizzard shuffled his papers and made to leave. 'We heard reports of a body being found by the crew of your police launch this afternoon. In the Haft, near the old fruit warehouse jetty, apparently. Any truth in that?'

'There was one, yes,' nodded Blizzard, 'although quite how you heard about it, I'm not sure. We've not released anything on it yet. Where did you find out about it?'

'Newsdesk got a call from some bloke who'd been walking his dog and saw your lot drag the body out of the water.'

'Those dog walkers, eh?' said the inspector with a slight smile. 'They get everywhere, don't they? Well, I can't tell you much about it, to be honest. All I can confirm is that we did recover a body.'

'Man, woman?'

'Yes.'

'Come on, Inspector,' protested the reporter. 'Give us something to go on.'

'OK. It was a man.'

'ID?'

'Not yet.'

'Cause of death?'

'We are not giving any information on that yet.'

'Is the discovery connected to any of your other inquiries?'

'It's far too early to talk about anything like that.' Blizzard stood up, the chair legs scraping on the floor. 'I'd love to stay and chat all day but that's your lot, I'm afraid. The Press Office will keep you informed of any developments. Angela is sitting at the back if you've got any questions.'

As the journalists headed for the door and the TV crews started dismantling their equipment, Blizzard walked across the room, rebuffed a couple of reporters' requests for further comment, and approached Ronald.

'Well handled,' said the superintendent approvingly, patting him on the shoulder. 'Very nicely done indeed. We'll make a media star of you yet.'

'Yeah, went well,' said Blizzard cheerfully. 'Not a bad day, all in all.'

Baz Garland closed his eyes and pulled the trigger.

Chapter Nineteen

THE TRAIN HAD only just rumbled out of the station and started to gather speed along the branch line when the bullet shattered the window of the carriage in which Katie Summers was sitting. For a second, the young detective stared in silent amazement at the only other person in the carriage, one of the businessmen she had seen on the platform. He gawped at the hole in the glass, just a matter of metres from his head, then exclaimed, 'What the—?'

'Quick,' said Summers, her police officer's instinct taking over. 'Get down in case there's another one.'

'Another what?'

'Another bullet.'

The comment shook the businessman to his senses and his features assumed a panic-stricken expression as he quickly did as he was told, crouching fearfully behind the seat, covering his head with his arms. Almost bent double, Summers made her way along the aisle until, at the far end of the carriage, and as the train began to slow down with a whine of brakes, she ventured a look out of the window. It took her a few moments to make anything out in the gathering mist and it was only when she looked behind the train that she saw to her horror that Baz

162

Garland had jumped down from the wire fence alongside the track and, having battled his way through the tangled mass of vegetation on the steep bank, had emerged onto the line. He was standing looking in the direction of the train, the familiar wild look in his eyes. Summers noticed with alarm that he was clutching a revolver, which he held down by his side.

'Shit,' she said, shrinking back into the carriage and gesturing to the businessman, who had started to stand up. 'Keep down, for God's sake.'

'Why? What's happening?'

'There's a lunatic with a gun on the tracks and, if he sees me, I'm a dead woman.'

'Jesus Christ!' The businessman had gone white and started to shake. 'Is he coming this way? Why's the train slowing down? What if he—?'

'Keep calm.'

Summers moved cautiously to the other side of the train and, peering out of the window, saw, to her relief, that Garland was squeezing through a gap in the fence on the far side of the tracks. As he did so, he looked round furtively and threw the gun into the bushes. Then he vanished into the street.

'It's OK,' said Summers with a sigh of relief as the train ground to a halt. 'He's gone.'

'Why was he after you?' asked the businessman, standing up and wiping the sweat from his brow with a handkerchief.

'Must have been something about the beer I served him,' said the constable drily, leaving behind the bemused businessman and feeling strangely calm as she jumped out of the carriage and started to run back to meet the two uniformed officers who had first confronted Garland and were now scrambling down the bank. Both looked shaken. Summers recognized one of them from the raid on the Lion the night before.

'It's Baz Garland!' she shouted and pointed. 'He dumped the gun over by that gap in the fence.'

'Cheers,' said one of the officers and they began to make off after him.

Summers was about to go with them when she noticed that a number of passengers had alighted from the carriages and were milling around looking bewildered and anxious. The young mother with the three children looked terrified and her youngest had burst into tears. The air was thick with the sound of wailing sirens now and Summers realized that her duty was to keep the situation under control. The last thing she wanted was frightened people wandering across the railway line, especially when she didn't know if other trains had been halted. Summers took the decision with a sense of relief; in her heart of hearts, she knew that she didn't want another confrontation with Baz Garland, gun or no gun. She'd had enough of him to last a lifetime. She never wanted to stare into those eyes again.

'I'm a police officer,' she said, trying to sound unconcerned as she took the crying toddler by the hand and ushered the passengers towards the bank. 'Come on, let's get off the line.'

They followed her without protestation and within a matter of minutes, the trackside was full of police officers. Summers saw a grim-faced Blizzard striding towards her from the direction of the station, David Colley in his wake, talking on his mobile phone. The chief inspector did a double take when he saw the constable standing by the carriage.

'What you doing here?' he asked. 'Hang on, don't tell me you were on the train?'

She nodded. 'I am afraid I was and I have to say that you're not doing very well on your promise to protect me from Baz Garland.'

'So it would seem,' said the inspector ruefully. 'You OK? Not injured?'

She shook her head. 'I'm fine. I saw Garland with a gun. He looked out of control. What happened?'

'Two of our lads tried to bring him in for threatening you. God knows where he got the weapon. None of our intelligence turned up anything to suggest that he had one. When they challenged him, he let off a shot. Went between them, thank God. Either he's a very good shot or a very bad one. I am trying not to think which one it was.' The inspector noticed the hole in the carriage window. 'It hit near you?'

'I was in the same carriage.' She gestured to the businessman, who was now sitting by the side of the track, still white-faced and wrapped in a blanket and shaking ever more vigorously as he was attended to by an ambulance officer. 'Closer to him, mind. A few feet further across and I reckon it would have hit him.'

'Lucky man.'

'Not sure he thinks so.'

'What was Garland up to, guv?' asked Summers. 'Why did he have a gun?'

'Not sure yet.'

'Do you think he was after me?' she asked quietly.

'Not sure.' Blizzard looked round to see Graham Ross appear round the end of the train, with the revolver in a plastic evidence bag. The inspector greeted his arrival with relief; the last thing he wanted to do was tell

Summers he thought she might have been the target. She had started to look anxious and he sensed that the tears were not far away again. 'Versace, what do we know?'

'Looks like old army issue,' said the forensics man. 'No wonder the bloody thing did not shoot straight, must be at least forty years old. I'll run a check when we get back, see if we can match it to any other jobs.'

'See if it matches the slug they picked out of George Rawcliffe while you're at it, yeah?'

'My first thought,' nodded Ross.

Before Blizzard could reply, the two uniformed officers walked down the track towards the detectives. Both were out of breath.

'You lose him?' asked Blizzard.

'Sorry, sir,' said one of them with a shake of the head. 'Gave us the slip. Never seen a man run like that. He's out of control.'

'OK, no problems. Listen, get yourself checked out with medics, will you? You've had a nasty shock.'

Blizzard turned to Colley as the officers walked towards a waiting ambulance.

'I want him picked up,' said the inspector urgently. 'Get everyone on it. Check all his haunts, track down all his associates. The last thing we want is Baz Garland running around the city in this mood.'

'Right-o.' Colley loped off down the track in the direction of the station.

Blizzard turned to Summers.

'Not sure we've done much to persuade you to stay,' he said with a slight smile. 'I suspect that anything I say now would be something of an insult.'

'It's definitely time to go home,' she said, noticing that her voice was trembling as her calm veneer continued to crumble.

'I suspect,' said the DCI, 'that you may be right.'

Chapter Twenty

A S DARKNESS FELL over Hafton, the sky was filled with the sound of wailing sirens and, across the city, the police fanned out in ever wider sweeps. Grim-faced fire-arms officers picked their way tentatively across playing fields and search teams smashed their way into derelict buildings, marched through housing estates, raided pubs, kicked down doors, established roadblocks and dragged people out of their homes for questioning. All the time over-head there came the constant clatter of the force helicopter, hovering low over deserted streets, its spotlight cutting a swathe through the gloom in the increasingly desperate search for Baz Garland. People stayed in their homes, kept their doors closed and prayed that the gunman would pass by silently in the night. Hafton was on lockdown.

Moving from street to street, back alley to back alley, Garland felt some of their fear as well. He knew that he had to get off the streets as quickly as possible but that he could not risk hiding out with friends, or even depend on them. Not now. The police would be banging on the doors of his associates and Garland knew that no one would want to be discovered harbouring a man who had fired a gun at police. He also realized that he'd be *persona non grata* among the city's villains, who would be cursing him;

everyone knew that, on something big like this, the police turned over stones that had lain undisturbed for years. Crouching in the shadows, Garland's biggest fear was that the city's gangland bosses would have sent out their own men to hunt him down and hand him over, probably after administering their own version of justice, in order to restore the delicate balance that existed between them and the police.

Not that Baz Garland regretted firing the gun; he'd said for years that he wanted to kill a police officer and he had meant it. His friends had always ignored the comments, blamed the drink, but burning deep within Baz Garland was a long-standing hatred that had become uncontrollable when he discovered that Katie Summers had betrayed him. He had borrowed the gun with just one thing in mind. His original intention had been to hunt down Summers but when the two uniforms confronted him, something had snapped in his mind. He'd felt it go, had felt light-headed, had noted with alarm a momentary bout of blurred vision. Now, his only regret was that he had missed them.

As Garland snuck through the streets, he could hear the police getting closer, caught occasional glimpses of officers through the darkness, their figures illuminated in the orange glow of the street lights, heard their voices as they searched for him. Somehow, and to his amazement, he managed to evade capture. Terrified at what they would do to him if they found him, his heart pounding and sweat glistening on his brow, he eventually made it as far as the bypass, sprinted across the road without being caught in the headlights and vanished onto the expanse of wasteland down by the Haft. Glancing nervously around, he saw to his relief that he had not been followed and started to limp slowly towards the river, his leg throbbing from the gash he had sustained as he leapt over the railway fence.

Garland did not have a plan, just knew that he had to find somewhere to hide, and find it quickly, somewhere the helicopter would not be able to pick him out with its searchlight. As he stumbled blindly through the darkness, he collided with a discarded barrel, his leg gave way and he crumpled to the ground with an agonized cry. Crouched on the wet earth, sobbing with the pain, his hand wet with blood as he examined the wound through torn trousers, he caught sight of the derelict fruit warehouse standing silent and skeletal a couple of hundred metres away. He knew the place well, had tried in vain to orchestrate a protest there when the owners announced its closure. Now, in what he realized was the ultimate irony, he was grateful that the place was unoccupied and, with a final glance back at the lights of the bypass, he struggled to his feet and dragged himself in the direction of the building.

Baz Garland's sense of fear was reflected in the front page of the newspaper placed on John Blizzard's desk by Arthur Ronald shortly after 6 p.m.

MASSIVE MANHUNT
FOR THE GUNMAN
POLICE LET GO

screamed the headline and next to it was a grainy black and white picture of the suspect with the caption: *'Baz Garland; freed by police and now named as the gunman who* fired at *officers'*.

'Marvellous,' sighed Blizzard, picking up the paper.

'They've rushed out a City Final special edition,' said

the superintendent, sitting down. 'They'll be absolutely bloody loving it. Press Office is run off its feet.'

'Everyone will be panicking now. Nothing like a deranged gunman on the loose to spook people.'

'Control room has been inundated with calls,' nodded Ronald. 'Frightened grannies mostly.'

The superintendent walked round the desk to look over his friend's shoulder at the newspaper. Garland's face stared back at him, the eyes wild as ever.

'Where do you think they got the picture?' asked Ronald.

'Looks like it's been blown up from one taken when the factory closed.'

'Funny how it always comes back to Smarts, isn't it?' said Ronald, sitting down again. 'Maybe you're right. Maybe all this is linked to the place.'

'And maybe it's not, Arthur. It's more likely to do with what happened at the Lion.'

'You pretty sure that Garland was going for young Katie, then?' Ronald looked at him sceptically. 'Surely, it was all hot air, those threats? The man's a gobshite, you said so yourself, you told her to ignore—'

'I know what I said, Arthur, but that was before he turned into Billy the Kid. I'm afraid that I've underestimated him all along.'

'You can't be too hard on yourself.'

'Can't I? I've just come off the phone from one of the DCs up in York – Micky Gray, used to work over in East. He heard what happened and wanted me to know that Garland did the same thing when he lived in York. Got obsessed about some young WPC who'd lifted him for assault on a picket line and made her life a misery for months. Went for her one night, tried to punch her. Waited outside the back door to the police station. She did not want to press charges but she had to transfer out of the city.'

'This just gets better and better,' sighed Ronald. 'I take it you got Katie away?'

'Traffic are giving her a lift. Oddly enough, she didn't fancy the train.'

Sitting in the back seat of the traffic car as it made its way through the city, Katie Summers watched in silence the flashing blue lights, the vans, the lights of the helicopter criss-crossing the city. Within a few minutes of leaving Abbey Road, the vehicle eased onto the dual carriageway and accelerated past the wasteland down by the river before speeding towards the motorway, towards Lincolnshire, towards another world. Once the car was clear of the city's western fringes, and even though there were two male officers sitting in the front, the young detective constable could not hold back the tears any longer.

Martin Bartholomew was standing at the window of his city-centre flat shortly before 6.30, staring down at the flashing blue lights in the street below, when his telephone rang.

'It's Roy,' said a voice when he picked up the receiver. 'Wanted to pick your brains.'

'About what?'

'I had a visit from a DCI Blizzard earlier today. Came to the university. Wondered if you knew him?'

'Not very well,' said Bartholomew, taking his cup of coffee and sitting down on the sofa. 'Why did he come to see you?'

'Don't play daft, you know exactly why. This Dennis

Smart business. He wanted to know about Henry Gallen. Seems he may be mixed up in it.'

'What's that got to do with you?'

'Don't play me for a fool, Martin. Blizzard seems to think that Gallen moved some money around for the Smarts directors and now he's found out that he came to the university. I assume he got it from you.'

'I might have mentioned it.'

'What exactly did you say?' asked the professor. Bartholomew sensed that he was trying to conceal his anxiety. 'Come on, Martin, I need to know what you told him.'

Bartholomew frowned. 'I should not really be talking to you about this, Roy. It's confiden—'

'I'll not tell anyone. Please, Martin, I need to know.'

'OK, between you and me, and to go no further, mind, I just told him that Henry was a student on one of your courses. That's all.'

'Nothing else?' asked Meehan.

'What else is there?'

There was a silence at the other end of the phone.

'Roy?' said Bartholomew after a few moments. 'You still there?'

'Sorry, Martin, it's just that your Mr Blizzard seems to have got it into his head that I am some sort of accessory to the crime. That what I taught Henry was what allowed him to commit the fraud. Such an allegation could be very damaging to both my reputation and that of the university and if Eastern Counties find out ... well, I do not need to tell you what might happen to the funding.'

'Yes, but surely you told him that you can't be responsible for what people do with the knowledge you give them?'

'Of course I did.'

'Then why are you worrying about it?'

'Blizzard did not seem to believe me. Between you and me, Martin, I don't think he's a particularly intelligent man. I was wondering if you could have a word with him? You know, explain the position?'

'I'm not sure that would be wise, Roy. Besides, I'm sure you have absolutely nothing to worry about. It was a course and that's all there is to it.'

Meehan gave a laugh which sounded forced to Martin Bartholomew.

'Yeah, you're right. Daft, really,' said the professor. 'Guess a visit from a detective can turn you paranoid. Thanks, Martin. Goodnight.'

'Night, Roy.'

The line went dead and a thoughtful Martin Bartholomew took a swig of coffee and walked across the room to his briefcase.

'Maybe I will have a word with Blizzard after all,' he murmured.

It was just past 6.30 when Dave Colley and Nick Towler got out of the sergeant's car, which he had parked outside the nursing home. It was the fifth address that they had checked in the search for Baz Garland since the shooting and, although neither expected to find him, there was always a chance that they'd locate Tommy Webb. He had not been at home nor in any of his usual watering holes and the detectives had remembered what they had heard about his seriously ill father.

Colley noticed a car parked nearby, fished a notebook out of his jacket pocket and flicked through the pages.

'Thought so,' he said, 'that's Tommy Webb's car. Oh, look, his tax disc is out of date.'

'Maybe another day, eh, Sarge?' said Towler. He looked at the ambulance parked on the driveway and recalled his previous visit to the home. 'Looks like the old man's an ill bunny. Looked pretty awful last time I was here. Not long for this world, if you ask me.'

'We seem to be pretty good at bursting in on deathbed scenes,' sighed Colley as they began to walk up the path. 'Something tells me I'm not going to make DI any time soon. More likely be joining Blizzard on school crossing duty.'

'More likely helping him get his sprog across the road.'

'Very inventive, Nick, skilfully worked in there, but it's unlikely to win you the whisky.'

The sergeant rang the bell. After a long wait, the door was opened by one of the staff, Colley showed his warrant card and, after a brief and heated discussion with the duty manager, the detectives were reluctantly ushered along a couple of corridors and through a lounge full of bored-looking pensioners sitting in front of a blaring television, which was showing news footage of the police search in Hafton. None of the residents showed any interest either in the television or the visitors. Leaving the lounge, the officers were led down another corridor and shown into a small, semi-lit room where several people were gathered silently around a bed, Tommy Webb among them.

'You lot seem to make a habit of this,' said a young blonde woman in a nurse's uniform, scowling at the officers as they walked in. 'Can't you see this is a bad time?'

'I'm genuinely sorry,' said Colley. 'I assume that you are Alison Rutter?'

She nodded and the sergeant looked at the pallid figure of her grandfather lying on the bed.

'I'm sorry for your loss,' he said, 'I really am.'

'He's not dead yet!' snapped Tommy Webb, glaring at him. 'Why are you here anyway? Can't you just leave us in peace?'

'I wish I could, Tommy, I really do, but we're trying to track down Baz Garland.'

'Well, he ain't here,' said Webb angrily. 'Why do you want him anyway? Don't tell me it's because of what he said to that bit of skirt?'

'I wish that's all it was about, Tommy,' said Colley, 'but it's more serious than that. I take it you've not heard that your friend tried to kill a couple of police officers this afternoon?'

Webb stared at him. 'He did what?'

'Shot at them. We need to find him quickly before he tries it again. This is a major criminal investigation.'

Webb's attention was distracted by a wheezing sound coming from his father followed by a rasping cough.

'You want to talk criminal?' said Webb through gritted teeth. 'Just look what those bastards did to my father!'

He stood aside and allowed the detectives to survey the old man. The twisted limbs, the sunken face, the dark-rimmed eyes.

'Just look, damn you!' he said.

Neither officer spoke. There did not seem to be the words.

'I know you don't want to hear this,' said Ronald, as Blizzard placed two mugs of tea on the desk, 'but the Smarts have been agitating. Making claims about violation of their human rights.'

'Damn, I clean forgot amid all the excitement!' exclaimed Blizzard.

Ronald shot him a look. 'Really?'

'OK, OK, I admit it, they've stewed enough,' admitted Blizzard, grimacing as he took a sip from his mug. 'Unlike this tea. No wonder Fee complains so much.'

Chapter Twenty-One

'LOOK, HOW MANY times, Chief Inspector?' sighed Margaret Smart. 'I didn't kill my husband. Nor did I kill George Rawcliffe. I mean,' – and she looked with exasperation across the interview-room table at Blizzard – 'do I really look the type to murder anyone?'

'In my experience, murderers seldom do.'

'You'll just have to take my word for it, then.'

'Well, someone killed them.'

'It wasn't me.'

Blizzard was tempted to agree. It was 8.30 that night and they had been in the stuffy little room for more than an hour, the inspector on one side of the desk and Margaret on the other, sitting next to her solicitor, a fastidious little man who had irritated the detective by constantly interrupting him. Not that the relationship between the two men would have been any better even if the lawyer had been silent; Blizzard had little time for solicitors. Never had, never would. The chief inspector eyed client and lawyer gloomily; the conversation had been going round in circles for a long time and he was beginning to think he was wasting his time.

'Look, Chief Inspector,' said the solicitor, 'my client has co-operated all that she can. She has admitted that she knew about the fraudulent activities at Smarts but that Jason Heavens and her husband were the brains behind them, along with her son and the accountant Henry Gallen.'

'Yes, I know she has said that but—'

'My client will plead guilty to fraud,' continued the lawyer, as Blizzard glared at yet another interruption, 'should the case ever come to court but she did not kill her husband and on that point she is most emphatic. She has told you repeatedly that she had no reason to wish him dead.'

'Yes, but what about the house? I mean, that must be worth—'

'You do seem to be clutching at straws, Chief Inspector, and from your line of questioning, I deduce that you have no evidence to suggest that my client committed either of these murders. For a start, I understand that you have witnesses that can place her in a shoe shop at the time her unfortunate husband was being pushed down the stairs.'

'She could have put someone up to it, though, and she did admit earlier in this interview that their relationship was not a loving one and—'

'Many marriages exist in a loveless atmosphere, Chief Inspector,' said the lawyer, 'but that does not mean that they all end in murder.'

'OK, I grant you that but neverthe—'

'Look, Chief Inspector,' said Margaret; her time to interrupt, 'my husband was not a pleasant man. He was cruel to Robert, he was cruel to most people, and, if I am brutally honest about it, I do not mourn his passing.'

'Margaret,' said the lawyer quickly.

'Mr Blizzard is no fool, Gerald, he knows what kind of a man my husband was and how he treated people. But I had nothing to do with the murders, Chief Inspector.'

'Let's assume I believe you,' said Blizzard. 'Any idea who might have wanted him dead badly enough to kill him?'

She hesitated.

'Margaret,' repeated Blizzard, leaning forward, sensing for the first time the sniff of a breakthrough. 'Do you know who did this?'

'There were phone calls,' she said quietly. 'Late at night.'

'Phone calls? What kind of phone calls?'

'Silent at first then later a voice, a man's voice, saying that we would pay for what we had done.' She shuddered.

'Did you assume he was talking about the fraud?'

'What else could it be?'

'Did the caller mention murder?'

'I only answered one of them, Dennis took the rest. He did not mention anything like that, though.'

'He could have been protecting you.'

'My husband, protecting me?' She gave a mirthless laugh. 'Let me tell you something, Chief Inspector. After we closed the factory and I started to hear about the effect it had had on people, I suggested to the others that we pay some form of compensation, that we owed it to these people. Do you know what my husband did? Do you?'

Blizzard watched in silence as Margaret lifted a hand to her cheek.

'He hit you?' said the inspector. 'For the benefit of the tape, Mrs Smart is nodding her head.'

'I hated him so much in that moment,' she said quietly.

'Enough to kill him?'

'Please, Chief Inspector,' said the lawyer, 'my client has already indicated that she did not murder her husband so the question is intrusive in the extreme.'

'Yes, thanks for reminding me, Mr Lloyd,' said the

inspector. 'What would we do without your noble profession keeping us right? Margaret, if we can get back to the phone call that you took. Did you recognize the voice?'

She shook her head.

'And your husband?' asked the inspector. 'Did he know who it was?'

'He did not say, if he did.'

'Does the name Baz Garland mean anything to you?'

'He was one of the men agitating trouble at the factory. Kept trying to get them out on strike. I only met him once, in the car-park. Nasty little man. Reeked of alcohol. He called me a fascist. Do you think he committed the murders?'

'I have no idea what to think, Margaret,' sighed Blizzard, sitting back in his chair. 'From what I can see they were queuing round the block to have a pop at you lot.'

He slid a piece of paper across the desk.

'Time to make a statement, I think,' he said.

The city clock had just struck nine in the distance when Baz Garland heard the voices. Limping over to one of the windows in the old warehouse, grimacing at the pain from his leg, he peered through the broken glass at the pinpricks of light that had appeared on the far side of the wasteland.

'Shit,' he murmured, slipped through a tear in the wall and started heading for the river.

'You'll like this,' said Colley, walking into the inspector's office a few minutes after nine, followed by Martin Bartholomew, 'especially given your enlightened views on our further education system.'

A weary Blizzard looked up from his paperwork and gestured for them to sit.

'Well?' he said, noticing Bartholomew's eager expression as he took his seat and the way that Colley was grinning. 'Someone tell me before you both burst.'

'I got a call from Roy Meehan earlier tonight,' said Bartholomew. 'He sounded really worried. Something just did not seem right. I felt it in my water.'

'Spoken like a true copper, Martin.'

'Thank you.' Bartholomew unclipped his briefcase. 'I think.' Bright-eyed, he produced a sheaf of papers which he placed on the inspector's desk. 'Look at that! I mean, just look at that!'

'Best you tell me what they say,' said Blizzard, eying the rows of blurred figures dubiously. 'Even if I could read them, I doubt I would understand what they said. What'cha find?'

'Well, it had always worried me about how Henry moved all that cash, see. He's a bright lad and all that, and the digital trail was clear enough, but I just was not sure that he was that bright. I mean, he's not as bright as me.'

'Ah, but does he have your modesty, Martin? Go on.'

'Well, the more I thought about it, the course he went on was pretty theoretical.'

'And?'

'And I came to the conclusion that he had to have had help.' Bartholomew looked at the documents. 'So I went back over everything we'd collected, reviewed the lot and—'

Blizzard sat forward, eyes bright, his fatigue banished. 'Please tell me what I think you're going to tell me,' he said. 'Oh, please do tell me that.'

Bartholomew did not need to speak. Colley's ever-widening grin said it all.

'Ah, but can you prove it?' asked Blizzard, tapping the documents.

'I can with a bit more work, yes,' nodded Bartholomew, 'particularly if I can get access to Roy's bank accounts tomorrow.'

'I am sure that can be arranged,' said Blizzard.

Sitting in the living room of his home, Roy Meehan shredded documents long into the night.

Shortly after ten o'clock, a considerably more cheerful inspector was back in the interview room, looking across the table at Robert Smart and his weasel-faced solicitor.

'This is a disgrace!' exclaimed the lawyer. 'My client has been held for more than twenty-four hours without interview and we will be making an official complaint—'

'Detective Superintendent Arthur Ronald,' said Blizzard affably. 'Extension 216, I think it is.' He glanced up at the clock. 'Although best leave it till morning, he'll be making his cup of Horlicks by now.'

'Your flippant attitude is hardly—'

'Let's cut through the cant, shall we, Mr Armitage?' said the inspector, a harsh edge to his voice. 'Your client is in it up to his neck. After this interview, he will be charged with fraud and, like as not, tax evasion charges will follow in due course. The CPS reckons with the evidence we've got he can expect a hefty prison sentence.'

'Henry Gallen!' exclaimed Smart. 'I knew the little bastard would snitch.'

'To be honest, we had it taped even before we lifted him. You could say it was child's play.'

'What does that mean?' asked the lawyer suspiciously.

'Electronic crime,' said the chief inspector, standing

up and walking round the room, 'is a rapidly developing branch of criminal activity and we, as a force, have embraced new forms of less traditional policing in order to ensure that we facilitate its detection.'

Smart and his lawyer stared at him in silence for a few seconds.

'I have no idea what you are talking about,' said the solicitor, as Blizzard sat down again, 'but I can assure you that my client will fight these charges all the way.'

'He'd be very foolish to do so. Not only do we have a digital trail, a phrase I learned tonight, oddly enough, which stretches as far as, where can we say, Robert? I know, Liechtenstein, how about that?' Blizzard paused to enjoy the startled expression on Smart's face. 'But your mother has also indicated that she will plead guilty.'

'You're bluffing!' exclaimed Robert.

''Fraid not.' Blizzard gave him a cheerful smile. 'Your mother's quite chatty when you get her in the right mood, isn't she?'

'My mother would not say anything to—'

'Don't be too sure. I got the impression that she was tired of it all. Wanted it all out in the open. Your mother also said that the family had been receiving threats.'

'She had no right to say that. It's family business.'

'Yes, and I appreciate that, as a family, you've been thick as thieves. Sorry,' said Blizzard, ignoring the glare, 'unfortunate choice of words, but I've got two bodies in the morgue and a chief constable who is very keen that I tell him who put them there. Now then, where were you when George Rawcliffe was killed?'

'At home.'

'Anyone verify that?'

'My whisky bottle. I got pissed. Eleanor can confirm it.

She had to pour me into bed.'

'Which brings us back to the threats, does it not? Any idea who they were from?'

Robert hesitated.

'My father recognized the voice,' he said at length. 'Not the first time, though, he reckoned the guy was trying to disguise it. My father worked it out on the second or third time. It was a guy who ran one of our suppliers, a little engineering firm down Gattle Street. Daft bastard tried to blame us for the death of his wife.'

'Edward Fothergill?'

'Yeah, that's him. My father said he'd sat in enough meetings with him whining on about not getting paid to know his voice anywhere. Besides, Henry said the guy went into The Red Lion from time to time and bad-mouthed us after he'd had a few.'

'Fothergill ever threaten to kill any of you?'

'No, nothing like that. I reckon he was the one behind the fires, mind. The first one happened a couple of weeks after his wife died.'

'You tell the police?'

'Oh, yeah,' said Robert with a dry laugh, 'you'd drop everything to help us, wouldn't you? We wouldn't be able to move for Neighbourhood Watch, would we? Besides, I sorted it myself. Didn't need you.'

'Meaning?' Smart hesitated. 'Come on, not much point in hiding things now, is there? It's all unravelling, in case you hadn't noticed. What did you mean by sorting it?'

Smart sighed. 'Henry put me in touch with a couple of lads from The Red Lion. They went round and he admitted making the calls but denied starting the fires. They gave him a reminder anyway.'

'I'll bet they did.'

'Robert,' said the solicitor, 'I really do not think it is wise to—'

'He'll find out anyway so why keep it secret?'

'I suggest you listen to your client, Mr Armitage,' said Blizzard, ignoring the lawyer's scowl. 'Does the name Baz Garland mean anything to you, Robert?'

'Good luck to him if it was him. Mad bastard.'

'Not quite the answer I was expecting.'

'Look,' said Smart, leaning forward, something about his demeanour suggesting that he had decided to unburden himself, 'let me level with you. When you came into the room when my father was dying? At the hospital? You were not intruding on family grief. Far from it.'

'I never thought I was.'

'None of us liked him. My father was a bully, a violent bully. He even struck my mother not long before he died and it was not the first time. Rawcliffe was the same, nasty piece of work, and I'm glad that they're dead but I did not kill them. I take it you've asked Garland about it? What'd he say?'

'Tried to murder two of my officers.'

'There you are, then.'

'Indeed,' said Blizzard gloomily. 'There we are.'

The clock had just ticked past eleven and the chief inspector was sitting in his office, his hands cradling the obligatory cup of lukewarm tea and his heavy-lidded eyes staring into the middle distance as his fatigue finally caught up with him. His phone rang, cutting into his reverie and making him spill his drink. With a muttered curse, he slammed his mug on the desk and picked up the phone.

'If it's bad news, I don't want to know,' he said grumpily.

'Sorry,' said Culley's voice; the sergeant sounded tired as well. 'We're at Edward Fothergill's. The place is in darkness and his car's gone. If you ask me, he flew the coop after I visited him. I don't reckon he's coming back.'

'OK,' sighed Blizzard. 'Add him to the APB list. Maybe we get money off for bulk.'

'Any news on Garland? Maybe he's left the city?'

'No, something tells me that he's still here, David. Nothing we can do about it now, though. Get yourselves away home.'

'Will do, although I suspect I've missed bath-time.'

'Something tells me that you have,' said the inspector.

'Wouldn't be the first time. Night, guv,' said the sergeant and the line went dead.

Blizzard snapped off his desk lamp, scooped his jacket off the back of his chair and walked with slow tread out into the deserted corridor. It had been a long day, as long as he could remember in his time as a police officer. The thought troubled him.

Shortly after 11.30, Baz Garland emerged warily from his hiding place in bushes alongside the river, shivering with the deepening chill of the night. Standing on the path, he glanced back nervously across the wasteland. The voices had faded some time previously but he had remained hidden until he was sure that the police search team had gone. The helicopter had swooped low over the river on one occasion since the officers had left, its spotlight strafing across the footpath and glinting off the brown waters of the Haft, but that had been an hour ago and he could hear it in the distance, reassuringly far away. Standing in the darkness of the night, all Garland could hear close by was the sound of cars on the bypass and, nearer, the lapping of the river. Feeling increasingly light-headed and with his leg having gone numb, he started to limp along the path, bound for he knew not where but knowing that he had to keep moving.

An hour later, finally back at home and slumped in his favourite armchair in the living room, John Blizzard drained his second glass of whisky and was about to stand up when Fee appeared at the door, dressed in her pyjamas and surveying him blearily.

'What time do you call this?' she asked.

'Too bloody late.' The inspector realized with a stab of guilt that, in the pressurized hours since the shooting, he had not given her and their unborn child a thought. 'You feeling OK?'

'I guess.'

'The little 'un?'

'Seems fine.'

Blizzard looked at her unhappily. 'Colley was talking about how he keeps missing Laura's bath-time,' he said. 'How can I do the job when the baby arrives, love?'

'We'll manage.' She perched on the arm of the chair and took hold of his hand. 'Trust me, John, we'll manage.'

'I wish I shared your confidence, I really do.'

'We'll make it work.'

'Yes, but look at today.' He glanced at the clock. 'This job, it takes everything you have.'

'Things will have to change, that's true. You'll have to make time for the baby as well.'

'I'm not sure I can.'

'You'll have to.'

'What if I can't?'

'Only you can answer that, John.' She rubbed her

swollen stomach. 'And judging by the amount of kicking that's going on, you have no more than a couple of days to do it.'

Shortly after midnight, the last flight of the day, the charter service from Malaga, broke through the clouds and touched down on the runway at a misty Hafton Airport where it taxied slowly to the rank and disgorged its cargo of returning holidaymakers. Among the lobster tans and the sombreros, a slim, smartly dressed man made his way down the aircraft's steps, pausing briefly once on the tarmac to shiver and pull his camel-hair coat around him before walking briskly to the terminal. Once inside the building, he calmly presented himself at passport control where one of the staff glanced without much interest at his documents and lazily waved him through to baggage reclaim.

When he was sure that the man was not watching, the officer turned to survey him, murmured 'Martin Crosby, my arse,' and picked up the phone.

'I'm looking to speak to DCI John Blizzard,' he said into the receiver. 'No? OK, will you get a message to him, please? Yes, it's urgent. Tell him that his eagle has landed.'

John Blizzard had just slipped into a fitful sleep haunted by images of Baz Garland's twisted features when the bedside phone rang.

Chapter Twenty-Two

'So,' said John Blizzard, tapping the pictures on the board behind him and surveying the officers gathered in the Abbey Road briefing room, 'these four lovelies are our main suspects for the murders. Have we missed anything?'

It was shortly after 8.30 the next morning and a frustrated chief inspector had summoned his twenty-strong investigation team to the briefing room to review the case. He'd been in early. After the message reporting the arrival of Jason Heavens at the airport, the inspector had briefed the force surveillance unit by phone – they had been waiting for his call for days – then managed to grab a few hours' sleep before waking up shortly before six, thoughts whirling round his mind. Realizing that further sleep was impossible as he lay there listening to Fee's gentle breathing and with his mind churning, the inspector had showered, grabbed a couple of slices of toast and driven into work, uncomfortably aware that the whiskies meant he was probably still over the limit but compelled to make the journey for all that.

As dawn broke grey over the sleeping city, he had sat in his office in the silent police station, feeling like the only man alive as he drank cup after cup of black coffee and brooded yet again over the lack of progress in the murder case, ever more convinced that he was trying to complete a jigsaw with a piece missing. He was also acutely aware that the longer he went without a breakthrough, the greater would become the pressure from headquarters. Blizzard knew that the release of Baz Garland was being seen by some as a blunder and, given his rocky relationship with the chief constable, blunders were the last thing he needed.

When the inspector had exhausted this gloomy line of thought, his mind strayed to the impending birth of his child and he replayed his conversation with Fee the night before. Life and death, he thought bleakly, and wondered not for the first time if he was really cut out to be a good father. Or a father of any type. The inspector had sighed heavily, determinedly pushed the thought to the back of his mind and tried once more to focus on the inquiry, inwardly cursing himself, just not sure for what.

Now, he stood before his team in the briefing room, seeking answers. Behind him were the pictures of four men. Heavens was one of the faces on the board, the grainy image staring back at the officers having been blown up from the newspaper cutting, the knowing smile still strangely unnerving for all it was indistinct. Next to him were the familiar twisted features of Baz Garland, again from the newspaper cutting, and beside him a picture of Edward Fothergill, removed from a frame in his house during a police search shortly after seven that morning. A mugshot of Robert Smart taken when he was arrested completed the gallery. Unable to hold him any longer, Blizzard had ordered him released the night before having been charged with fraud.

'Let's start,' said the inspector, looking to his team,

'with the links. See if we can find anything new because everywhere I turn I run into another dead end and it's making my head hurt. 'Course that could be the whisky when I got home last night.'

'You didn't win the sweepstake, did you?' said Colley. 'That's got to be cheating.'

The others laughed and so did John Blizzard. It felt good to enjoy humour and the experience lifted some of the gloom from his mind.

'OK,' he said, waiting for the room to fall quiet then turning serious and looking again at the pictures. 'Anyone fancy having a go? What links them? Anything?'

'The factory,' said Nick Towler. 'Smarts. I know it's obvious, guv, but it's the one thing that connects them all.'

'Obvious and important,' nodded Blizzard. 'OK, so they're all part of the Smarts story but two did well out of the company's demise and two were left with good reason to feel aggrieved, which would seem to put them on different sides of the equation.' He tapped the pictures of Garland and Fothergill. 'An alliance?'

'Can't see that,' said Towler. 'Fothergill was a boss and Garland is a rabid union guy. An unholy alliance, if ever there was one, and Baz Garland does not come over as the type to compromise on his principles.'

'No, he doesn't,' said Graham Ross. 'What's more, ballistics say that the bullet that the pathologist pulled out of Rawcliffe does not match the one that we recovered from the railway line. And when we searched Fothergill's house we found nothing of use. We can't even connect him to the fires.'

'And even if you did,' said Colley dubiously, 'he didn't strike me as the type to kill anyone. Wanted to get back at them, yes, I buy that, but prepared to kill for it? Sorry, but

I don't see it.'

'My money's on Heavens anyway,' said Towler. 'Where is he, by the way?'

'That little hotel on McNay Street,' said Blizzard. 'Under the name Martin Crosby. He's not left his room since checking in.'

The police surveillance officer shifted uncomfortably in his seat and winced at the discomfort in his right leg; he'd been sitting in the back of the white van for the best part of eight hours, his eyes fixed on the monitor ever since, at dead of night, he and his colleague had pulled up in McNay Street. He glanced across at his fellow officer, who was staring at the screen while sipping from a plastic cup. Draining the cup, he reached for a flask, held it up, watched the remaining drops fall out.

'Empty,' he said. 'Just as well, since I need a slash.'

'Heathen,' said his colleague.

'Why Jason Heavens, Nick?' asked Blizzard, looking at Towler, then at the faces on the board. 'Why him?'

'Well, just because he was not in the country at the time of the murders does not rule him out, does it?' said the constable. 'Your original falling-out-among-thieves theory, guv.'

'Yeah,' nodded Colley. 'It would be easy enough to arrange a hit from Spain. There's enough expat criminals out there. Remember when me and Gibbo went out to Fuengirola to lift Matty Hooper? You couldn't move for bad lads.'

'And I'll bet Heavens has got access to those kind of people,' nodded Towler. 'I'll bet he moves in those kind of circles.'

'And even if he didn't bring in a pro,' said Colley, warming to the theme, 'maybe he put Robert up to it. Robert would not have needed much persuading, I suspect. He made it abundantly clear that he hated his father, didn't he?'

'Trouble is, he has an alibi for that one,' said Blizzard, adding thoughtfully. 'Could be fake, I guess. What do you think, David, you talked to the council guy?'

'I guess I didn't exactly put the thumbscrews on.'

'Hang on,' said Ross. 'If all they wanted was the money, this Gallen fellow could have moved it sitting at his desk, couldn't he? Why go to the trouble of killing people? And why aren't the women on the board, guv? What if Margaret and Eleanor are in on it?'

'And Tommy Webb for that matter?' added Towler. 'And that daughter of his? Alison Rutter. Revenge is a pretty powerful motive, we all know that.'

He looked at the others, who nodded. Blizzard turned back to the pictures on the board.

'Whichever way I look at it, it just does not make any sense,' he said.

'Hey up,' said the surveillance officer, sitting forward in his seat as the screen showed the hotel door swing upon and a slim man in a camel-hair coat walk briskly down the stairs. The man glanced up and down the street but took no notice of the white van with *D Bartle and Son, Decorators* painted on the side.

'Heavens,' said the surveillance officer and reached for his radio.

'Anything to add, Chris?' asked Blizzard, looking at his DI.

'Lincolnshire,' said Chris Ramsey. He had not

contributed to the discussion and had hardly spoken since he had walked into the briefing room, clutching several brown files, and sat down at a desk where he proceeded to pore over them. 'It might be nothing, mind.'

'Even then it would be better than what we have,' said Blizzard. 'What you got?'

'Well, these,' and Ramsey held up the files, 'contain most of what we know about the Smarts directors. According to this Companies House record that the fraud boys unearthed, Dennis Smart, Heavens and Rawcliffe were once the co-owners of a holiday chalet park in Skegness.'

'Skeggy,' said Blizzard wistfully. 'Had some cracking family holidays there when I was a kid. I reckon we'll take the little 'un there when it's big enough.'

The others smiled at the thought.

'Yes, I can just see you in a Kiss Me Quick hat,' said Ramsey.

Everyone stared at him; the detective inspector did not have a reputation as a humorist but had made several jokes in the past forty-eight hours.

Blizzard chuckled. 'I guess not,' he said. 'I take it that they don't own the place now?'

'No. It seems that they sold it five years ago. There's another document which seems to suggest that they got the thick end of five million pounds for it. Place was a little gold mine, apparently.'

'It would be,' nodded Blizzard. 'Very popular with the hoi polloi, is Skegness. Did Fraud Squad not think it was relevant, Chris?'

'Apparently not.'

'But you think it might be?'

Ramsey shrugged. 'It's all I've got.'

'Looks like our Katie is not finished with the inquiry after all,' said Blizzard.

'It's probably nothing,' said Ramsey.

She walked down the corridor and hesitated at the top of the staircase, her heart pounding in her ears, her hand clammy as it gripped the banister. She knew instinctively, knew without even knowing how, that she was not alone in the building. Realized with a sick feeling that this was the moment she had expected, the moment she had dreaded for days. Not normally a woman prone to fear, she felt cold as she stood at the top of the stairs.

Standing and looking down at the hallway, she tried to retain her composure. She peered in vain for movement in the half-light, strained to hear any sound which would identify the location of the intruder. Something that would give her the edge. Nothing stirred and she stood for the best part of a minute listening to the silence of the building. When it came, though, the noise was behind her.

She tensed as she heard someone walking slowly down the corridor towards her. Then the breathing. Close. Heavy. Familiar from her nightmares. Afraid to confront her killer, she continued to stare down into the hallway as if fascinated by something on the floor.

'Don't turn round,' said a voice she knew well.

'Why?' She tried to sound calm although her trembling voice betrayed her. 'You scared to face me?'

'Always the melodramatic type, weren't you?' A sneer in the voice.

'Melodramatic? After what you did?' Anger. 'I trusted you and you....'

Her voice tailed off and she glanced sideways and caught a glimpse of the intruder in the wall mirror.

She made not a sound as her assailant lunged at her. Did not have time to react, so sudden was the movement. A shove in the back sent her crashing down the stairs. She momentarily appeared to hang in the air, a life in slow motion, a death in freeze-frame, until time resumed and she continued to fall. She struck her head three times on the banister and hit the floor with a crunching sound, the impact twisting her leg at a sickening angle. As her killer walked down the stairs, stepping over her broken body and out through the front door, closing it with the quietest of clicks, she lay silent, blood oozing from an ugly head wound, her lifeless eyes staring up at the ceiling.

Shortly after 9.30, the phone rang in the CID Room and Summers picked it up; it was good to be back in the old routine.

'It's Blizzard,' said the voice at the other end. 'How do you fancy a trip to the seaside? I've cleared it with your gaffer. Nick Towler's on his way over.'

The inspector was still smiling when he replaced the receiver. As he did so, Colley walked into the office.

'How she take it?' asked the sergeant.

'Like I'd asked her to kill her firstborn.'

'Very good,' said Colley approvingly, taking a piece of paper from his jacket pocket and glancing at the clock. 'Three and a half seconds, I make it. Maybe you'll be able to enjoy that whisky after all. Pass me a pen, will you? Oh, the surveillance boys have been on. Jason Heavens is on the move.'

'Game on,' said Blizzard, standing up. 'I just wish I knew the rules.'

Sprawled out under old sheeting in a corner of the derelict

building, Baz Garland groaned and opened his eyes to find himself staring into the barrel of a gun.

'Hello, Baz,' said the armed officer. 'Fancy a walk?'

Three miles away, Professor Roy Meehan had just parked his vehicle in the university car-park when a police patrol vehicle pulled up, out of which emerged a young woman and a uniformed male officer.

'Professor Roy Meehan?' said the woman, walking up to him and producing a warrant card. 'DC Jeffers from Abbey Road Police Station CID. I wonder if you would mind accompanying me, please?'

'Why?' Meehan tried to look unconcerned even though his heart had started to pound.

'My DCI Mr Blizzard would like a chat with you.'

'But I've done nothing wrong, I told him that yesterday,' said Meehan, starting to walk towards the building only to find his way barred by the uniformed officer. The professor tried to brush past him but the officer took hold of his arm.

'Don't make this more difficult than it needs to be,' said Jeffers, coming to stand beside the professor as a number of teenagers stopped to watch the confrontation. 'I would hate for you to make a scene in front of your students. Wouldn't exactly be good for the reputation of the university, would it?'

Meehan noticed the watching students and, trying to make it look as if he was going voluntarily, he nodded and began to walk towards the police vehicle. 'What does he want to talk to me about anyway?'

Jeffers gave a slight smile.

'Electronic Crime in a Post-Capitalist Age,' she said.

Chapter Twenty-Three

'WELL, BAZ,' SAID Blizzard, back in the interview room that afternoon and surveying the dishevelled figure slumped opposite him, 'you *have* led us a merry dance.'

Although Garland had spent more than two hours under armed guard at the General Hospital following his arrest, his face was still dirty, his hair lank and unkempt, and his left arm was trembling. He did not reply to the inspector's comment but stared at him out of dulled eyes; it seemed to the detective that the fire had gone from him. There was something – Blizzard cast around for the right word – something *disappointing* about the man who now faced him.

In a strange way, Blizzard had relished his encounters with Garland, appreciated his passion and his anger, enjoyed the challenge of an adversary who said what he thought. When the thought had first came into his head as he watched Garland being brought into the custody suite twenty-five minutes previously, the inspector had been surprised by the idea but now that he had had time to think about it, he could rationalize the feeling. With the likes of the Smarts directors there were secrets, veils of deceit, a cruelty which was callous and premeditated, a dark heart beneath an outwardly respectable veneer, the same with Henry Gallen and Roy Meehan; but with Garland, you got what you saw and the inspector found that strangely refreshing. He suspected that Garland had been called many things in his time but never refreshing and certainly not now as a fetid odour rose rank and stale from his filthy body and filled the interview room.

'I think,' said Garland's lawyer, wrinkling his nose at the stench from the prisoner, 'that, in the circumstances, it would make sense to conclude proceedings as rapidly as possible. My client would be prepared to broker a deal with you, Chief Inspector.'

'I'm not sure he looks capable of brokering anything, Mr Archer.' Blizzard spoke equably to the solicitor; Philip Archer was one of the few lawyers in the city for whom he had respect. Different from Garland in every way but nevertheless also a man who concealed no secrets, the inspector had always thought. 'But anything that gets us out of this room before he stinks the place out would be welcome.'

'Indeed so. Having taken instruction from him, I am authorized to tell you that he is prepared to plead guilty to attempting to shoot your officers when the case comes to court.'

'Well, since he was standing in front of them brandishing a gun like Wild Bill Hickok, I'm not sure he has much in the way of alternatives.'

'My client appreciates that. However, I must warn you that he will not plead guilty to attempted murder, rather to a charge that reflects the fact that the balance of his mind was disturbed at the time of the incident.'

Blizzard nodded; he had expected the lawyer to suggest something of that ilk and, after seeing Garland's condition, the inspector had come to the same conclusion himself, if reluctantly. Indeed, he had decided, were he to ever find himself in the same position, he'd probably do the same thing.

'I suspect we will have to let the court decide that,' he said, deciding not to share his opinions with the lawyer, 'although our inquiries have turned up several associates prepared to testify that your client has threatened to kill police officers on a number of occasions. Is that not right, Baz?'

Garland stared at him without emotion and said nothing.

'Words,' said the solicitor. 'They were just words, Chief Inspector.'

Shortly before three that afternoon, Katie Summers and Nick Towler met up at the police station in a bleak Skegness and drove to the outskirts of the town where, as the houses gave way to muddy fields shrouded in gathering mist, they found the holiday chalet park closed and silent, the happy cries of children and the bustle of the holiday season already a distant memory of a lost summer. The officers got out of the car and walked up to the main gates, which were padlocked. Towler looked round at the dank woodland which fringed the site.

'Who'd come here for a holiday?' he said.

'Looks like you've had a wasted journey,' said Summers, as she peered through the wire fence.

'Actually, it might not have been wasted after all.' Towler pointed to a man walking his dog in between the chalets. 'Hey!'

Man and dog came towards them.

'What do you want?' grunted the man suspiciously as he approached the gate.

'Police,' said Summers, flashing her warrant card. 'We're conducting some inquiries on behalf of CID in Hafton.'

The man nodded and unlocked the gates. Katie Summers glanced at Nick Towler; it seemed to both officers that something had changed in the man's demeanour at mention of the word Hafton.

'I understand,' continued Philip Archer, looking across the desk at Blizzard, 'that the last time you had my client in for interview you suggested that he might have been involved in the murders of two of the directors of Smarts?'

'He's certainly a person of interest,' nodded Blizzard, 'although I suspect you're going to tell me that he should not be. Every other bugger has denied it.'

'My client may be guilty of many things, Chief Inspector, but there is nothing to connect him to these offences and I must warn you that any attempt to—'

'No need to warn me about anything. I agree with you.'

'You do?' The solicitor looked genuinely surprised. 'I would have thought that in the circumstances you would have been tempted to pin—'

'Philip,' protested the inspector, 'Philip, how long have we known each other?'

'Fifteen years.'

'And in all that time have you ever known me to "pin" anything on anyone?'

Archer held up his hands.

'I apologize,' he said, and glanced at the hunched figure of Baz Garland. 'An unfair comment. Perhaps I can atone by telling you that my client is prepared to admit to his involvement in a series of arson attacks at the Smarts factory?'

'He is?'

'Yes, he is. Although, I should say that he is not prepared to be held solely responsible and would seek to implicate two other men in the offences.'

'Is one of them Edward Fothergill, by any chance?'

The lawyer glanced down at his notepad. 'I have no idea who he is,' he said. 'No, I am referring to Ronald Maskell and a man called Thomas Webb. They did them together to get back at the management, according to my client.'

'Figures.'

'To be honest, I thought you'd look more pleased, Chief Inspector. I rather thought that I might be doing you a favour.'

'You are.'

'Then why the long face?'

Blizzard sighed. 'I seem to be solving every crime except the one I'm supposed to be investigating,' he said. 'I've never come across a case in which so many people are innocent. You don't happen to have any clients who might be prepared to put their hand up to murder so I can get home, do you?'

The owner of the chalet park, a balding middle-aged, scruffily dressed man by the name of Donald Carlew, took the detectives to a two-storey brick building where he ushered them through a shabby ground-floor pool room, the tables covered with grubby green baize, the bar in darkness and the air musty and damp. He led them upstairs into a cluttered office, its threadbare carpet littered with cardboard boxes.

'Apologies,' he said without sounding sorry. Carlew sat down behind the desk. 'Off-season, having a clear out. How can I help you?' He reached for a mug, discovered that the contents were cold, scowled and headed for the kettle in the corner of the room. 'Tea?'

They nodded.

'We want to know something about the previous owners of this place,' said Katie Summers as Carlew busied himself with his tea-making.

'I assumed you did.'

'You did?'

'I heard that Smart and Rawcliffe were dead. The radio said they'd been murdered so I guessed you'd come calling eventually.'

'You bought this place from them, I think?' said Towler.

'Yeah,' nodded Carlew. 'There was three of them. A chap called Jason Heavens as well. Strange bloke. Bought it from them a couple of months after the accident.'

'Accident?' said Summers. 'What accident?'

'Surely you know about that?' Carlew turned round, a box of teabags in his hand. 'The girl as fell down the stairs? I assumed that's why you're here.'

Blizzard had just returned from the interview with Garland, and was sitting at his desk in his office making notes, when there was a knock on the door and Arthur Ronald walked in.

'Making any progress?' asked the superintendent, the chair creaking as he sat down.

'Not on the murders,' said Blizzard, putting down his pen. 'There's something we don't know here, Arthur, I'm sure of it. Last piece of the jigsaw. Garland has coughed to the fires, though, which is something, I guess.'

'But not to the killings?'

Blizzard shook his head. 'His lawyer is adamant that he's innocent.'

'And you believe him?' asked Ronald.

'Oddly enough I do.'

'Even after what Garland tried to do to our officers?'

Before the chief inspector could say anything else, David Colley walked into the room.

'Surveillance have been on,' he said. 'Heavens is on the move. They can't be sure but they reckon he might have a gun.'

Blizzard stood up and fished his coat down from the back of the door.

'Come on,' he said, striding out into the corridor, 'time to finish this once and for all, I think. I just wish I'd thought to look at the picture on the lid before I started out.'

Colley looked at Arthur Ronald in bemusement.

'Jigsaws,' explained the superintendent.

'Ah,' said Colley. 'Another of his little sayings.'

Katie Summers looked sharply at the chalet-park owner.

'Fell down the stairs?' she said. 'When was this?'

'Five years ago. I bought this place in the November.' Carlew poured the hot water into a grubby teapot. 'They seemed in a real hurry to get rid of it. The estate agent reckoned I'd have to pay six mill but they settled for just under five. I wasn't surprised, really, it was a nasty business. Police all over the place. Folks asking questions. I'd have wanted to get out of it, too.'

He poured the teas and placed the mugs on the desk.

'So what happened to the girl?' asked Towler. 'How come she fell down the stairs?'

'Well, I weren't living round here at the time so I have to go on what I have picked up from the locals. The girl, she was a cleaner, summer job. Sixteen or seventeen, I think. They allus used younger girls, cost them less.' Carlew sat down behind his desk. 'Word was there was some kind of party after the season ended. A thank-you to the staff. Downstairs in the pool room.'

'Who was there?' asked Towler.

'The owners came down from Hafton, and some of the girls who worked for them, they were there as well. Some of the locals reckon that the men got the girls drunk. Not so sure Heavens would be into that but I can see Rawcliffe and Dennis Smart doing it. Nasty pieces of work, they were, and folks reckon Rawcliffe had a thing for underage girls. There was talk of them having sex with some of the girls but nowt that could be proved. A few days later, one of the girls were found at the bottom of the stairs.'

'Found by who?'

'Jason Heavens, I think. Her neck was broked, I heard.'

The late-afternoon mist was also starting to shroud Hafton when John Blizzard's Granada pulled up on a road running through a newly built housing estate fringing the northern edge of the city. On one side of the road were neatly kept semi-detached houses, their clipped lawns and weed-free drives a stark contrast to the large expanse of wasteland standing opposite. Once a thriving enamel works, now the site was an area of scrubland across which were interspersed the few scraggy bushes and forlorn trees that could survive on soil still bearing evidence of contamination from the plant's heyday. AVAILABLE FOR DEVELOPMENT said a faded sign rather optimistically; it looked like it had been there for years. The inspector parked behind a white van and the detectives got out and approached the vehicle. Blizzard knocked twice on the back door, which swung open to let them in.

'Where is he?' asked Blizzard of the two surveillance men as the detectives clambered in.

'There's a ruined old building about halfway across,' said one of them.

'I know it,' nodded Blizzard. 'Used to be a workshop. Heavens in there?'

'Yup.'

'What's he doing?'

'Seems to be waiting for someone.'

'He definitely got a gun?'

'We're not so sure now,' said the surveillance man. 'We thought he was carrying something under his coat when he left the guest house but it might be nothing. The armed guys are on their way just in case. What do you want to do?'

'If he's waiting for someone, so will we,' said the inspector. 'I've waited long enough for him, a few more minutes won't harm.'

'They said it was an accident, of course,' continued the chalet-park owner, taking a sip of tea. 'Said that she were cleaning this office and must have slipped at the top of the stairs. That was their story, anyhow.'

'But you're not sure?' said Towler.

'Folks talk. That's all I'm saying.'

'Did the police investigate?' asked Summers.

'Yeah, but they found nothing. Folks reckon that the place had been tidied up. Police didn't turn up so much as a beer can. The inquest agreed that it were an accident and that were that. I mean, folks can talk, pub talk and that, but it doesn't necessarily mean anything, does it? You know what gossip's like. You must hear a lot of it in your line of work.'

Nick Towler recalled the way that Blizzard had refused to ignore the chatter and had always held true to his belief that there was more to the closure of Smarts than met the eye.

'Sometimes it pays to listen to it,' said Towler.

'Yeah, well, whatever the truth of it, your lot never charged anyone with owt. Case closed. A few weeks after the kid died, the For Sale sign went up and I bought it at a knock-down price.' Carlew grinned then downed the last of his tea. 'Every cloud, eh?'

'I've had enough of this,' said Blizzard, glancing at his watch after an hour. 'Let's lift Heavens before we lose the light altogether.'

Within a couple of minutes, armed police officers made their way carefully across the wasteland and converged on the old red-brick workshop, which stood dark and silent close to a bedraggled copse, its skeletal form dimly illuminated by the orange glow from the street lights that had started to come on nearby as dusk fell. Blizzard and Colley followed behind the armed teams while, back on the street, uniformed officers held back the crowds that had started to gather as local residents came out of their homes to watch events unfold.

'Armed police!' shouted one of the firearms officers when he was close enough to the building. 'Jason Heavens, come out with your hands in clear view!'

There were a few moments of silence.

'Jason Heavens!' repeated the officer. 'We have the building surrounded. Come out with your hands in clear view!'

There was a further period of silence then the door to the workshop grated open and Heavens appeared. Seeing that several marksmen had their sights trained on him, he held his hands up to show that he was not carrying a weapon. He spotted Blizzard behind the armed officers.

'We must stop meeting like this, Chief Inspector,' shouted Heavens, the usual knowing smile on his face.

'Jason Heavens,' said Blizzard, walking up to him after officers had searched him and confirmed he was not carrying anything, 'it gives me great pleasure to arrest you for fraud.'

'Fraud?' He seemed genuinely surprised. 'You not going to pin the murders on me?'

'You're the second person who's said that to me today, Jason. I take it you're denying all knowledge? Every other bastard has.'

'Murder is not my style, Chief Inspector,' said Heavens, as the handcuffs went on. 'You know that as well as I do. As for the fraud, my lawyer will get me out of that one easily enough. I'll blame the others.'

'You can try.'

'Come on, Chief Inspector,' said Heavens as Blizzard started to lead him across the wasteland. 'Juries are stupid, you know that. Half of them can't even spell their own name so what do you think they'll make of a complicated fraud case after a smooth-talking lawyer has talked at them for three weeks? It all comes down to whether they like the look of the man in the dock and my suits are as sharp as you can get. I have an excellent tailor, you know.'

'You keep thinking that,' said Blizzard, as they reached the street, but he knew that Heavens was right.

'This girl,' said Katie Summers, looking across the desk at Carlew. 'What was her name?'

'Amy something. Can't remember her surname. Hang on, though, there was a newspaper cutting. From the inquest.' He walked over to the filing cabinet and searched through one of the drawers. 'Ah, here you are, not sure why I kept it, really.'

He handed the cutting to Katie Summers.

'Well?' said Towler as she read the story. 'What was her name?'

'Gallen,' said Summers quietly. 'Amy Gallen.'

Blizzard's mobile rang as the uniforms began to take Jason Heavens towards a waiting van.

'Blizzard,' said the inspector, having taken the phone from his coat pocket.

'It's Katie.' She sounded excited. 'The killer, I think it's Henry Gallen. He believes they killed his sister.'

Hearing a noise from the crowd, Blizzard turned round to see that a figure had forced his way through the police cordon and was walking slowly towards the van. He was holding a handgun.

'I think you could be right,' said the inspector. He slipped the phone back into his pocket.

'Don't come any closer,' said Gallen, noticing the police officers walking across the wasteland. 'I have no argument with any of you. My argument is with him.'

He pointed the gun at Heavens, who stared at him in horror, the smile wiped from his face for the first time that the inspector could remember. The onlookers panicked, turned and fled, the air full of their screams and, within moments, the street was all but deserted. Blizzard held up his hands to show that he was unarmed.

'We know about your sister, Henry,' he said. 'We know about Amy.'

'He killed her,' said Gallen as he gestured to Heavens. 'Him and the others.'

'It was an accident,' said Heavens quickly.

'Clearly, Henry does not think so,' said Blizzard.

'It was no accident! They killed her!' exclaimed Gallen, close to tears now, his hand trembling as he struggled to keep the gun pointing at Heavens.

Blizzard glanced at Heavens.

'Well?' said the inspector. 'Do you not think he deserves an explanation, Jason?'

'OK, OK,' sighed Heavens, 'but it was not me who did it. Smart and Rawcliffe, they were the ones. It was Smart who pushed her.'

'Yes, but you could have stopped him,' said Gallen, his voice quivering. 'You could have stopped it, Jason. She trusted you. The family trusted you.'

Blizzard noticed that one of the firearms officers, standing further back on the scrubland, out of Gallen's eyeline, had moved round until he could fix the gunman in his sights. The inspector knew that events were out of his hands now; protocol dictated that, if the firearms officer thought that Gallen was about to fire, he would drop him where he stood. Blizzard knew he had but seconds to avert another death.

'We can sort this out, Henry,' he said. 'We can help you get justice for your sister.'

'I've already done that.' Gallen jabbed the gun towards Heavens again. 'He's the last of them.'

'Don't you want someone to stand trial, though? Have your sister's story told at last?' asked Blizzard.

Gallen hesitated.

'Come on, Henry,' said Blizzard. 'Give me the gun. Let's end this.'

Blizzard glanced to his left and saw the firearms officer's trigger finger tightening. Gallen followed his gaze and noticed the officer for the first time.

'If he pulls that trigger, you will die,' said Blizzard, 'and nothing I can say will stop him. You can be sure of that.'

'I don't care.' Gallen gestured to Heavens with his gun. 'As long as he's dead.'

'Then who will tell your sister's story?' said Blizzard, talking quickly now. 'Who will stand up in court to take her side, Henry? Only Jason can tell us what really happened and if you kill him—'

'I've got Amy's diary. That will tell her story. I don't need him.'

'But it won't talk about the murder, will it?' said the inspector. 'There's only one man alive who can tell us what really happened to Amy and, if you kill him, we'll never know, will we?'

Gallen glanced again at the motionless firearms officer with his weapon trained on him.

'I don't know,' he mumbled.

'Listen, Henry,' said Blizzard. 'I promise that he'll pay for what he's done. You have my word on that.'

The inspector gave him what he hoped was a reassuring smile. Gallen stared at the detective for a moment, the man he feared above no other, and came to a sudden decision. He nodded, dropped the gun and stood still, shoulders heaving as he sobbed and the uniforms engulfed him. A smattering of applause could be heard from those people who had stayed to watch the drama unfold from a safe distance.

'Thank you,' said Heavens. 'I owe you one.'

'Don't thank me, Jason,' said Blizzard. 'I'm going to make sure that they lock you up and throw away the key, smooth-talking lawyer or not.' He nodded at one of the uniformed officers.

'Get him out of my sight,' he said.

As Heavens was bundled into the van, Colley walked up

to the inspector and touched him lightly on the shoulder.

'That smile's coming on nicely,' he said.

Shortly after 6 p.m. a dishevelled man walked up the steps to Abbey Road Police Station and presented himself to the officer on reception.

'I wonder if I could talk to Detective Sergeant Colley?' he said.

'Certainly, sir, I'll see if he's available. Who are you?'

'Fothergill,' said the man. 'Edward Fothergill.'

Chapter Twenty-Four

'So how did you find out what they did to her?' asked Blizzard as, that evening, he and Colley looked across the interview-room table at the hunched figure of Henry Gallen, sitting next to the lawyer Philip Archer. 'The diary?'

Gallen nodded.

'When was this?' asked the inspector.

'Just over a month ago.' Gallen was struggling to keep his voice steady. 'I knew nothing about what had really happened before then. None of us did. Never even suspected.'

'How come it took you so long?'

'No one knew the diary existed. After Amy died, I brought her stuff back in a suitcase and took it to my mother's. Mum could not bring herself to open it; she'd kept her bedroom untouched and no one was allowed to go in there, so the case sat unopened until Mum died.'

'Which was when?'

'Earlier this year. Cancer. We sold the house and the case came to me. Sat for months in the spare room.'

'But you opened it eventually?' said Blizzard.

'I got drunk one night. Found the diary and started to read. Couldn't stop. I could hear her voice as I read.' Gallen shook his head. 'I had no idea. I'd always believed them when they said it was an accident. Everyone did. We had no reason to think otherwise.'

'How come your sister was working at the chalet park in the first place?' asked Colley. 'It's a fair trek from Hafton.'

'She wanted a summer job to earn some extra cash. She was saving up for a car. Robert mentioned it to Rawcliffe and he offered her some summer work. I thought they were doing us a favour. Amy was not sure about it at first but I told her it would be fine.' Gallen turned haunted eyes on the detectives. 'I sent my little sister to her death. Do you know what that feels like?'

'I'm not sure any of us can know what that feels like,' said Blizzard. 'What exactly did the diary say?'

'At first it was all about how much she enjoyed working there and was looking forward to the end-of-season party. Thought it would be a bit of fun.' Gallen gave a mirthless laugh. 'A bit of fun. Didn't quite turn out like that, did it?'

And Henry Gallen started to cry.

'It was just supposed to be a bit of fun,' said Heavens, staring across the table at the two detectives. He seemed keen to tell his side of the story now and his composure had returned. 'That's all. A bit of fun to thank the boys and girls who'd worked the summer for us. I did not think anything would happen.'

'But you knew what Rawcliffe and Smart were like, Rawcliffe particularly,' said Blizzard. 'You knew he liked young girls. You bear as much responsibility for this, Jason.'

'I am not sure my client can be held responsible for the behaviour of others, Chief Inspector,' said his lawyer quickly.

'But she was only a kid,' said Blizzard, the strength of his emotional response surprising him. 'Her family trusted you to look after her and you abused that trust.'

'Maybe so,' said Heavens, 'but she was old enough to know better.'

'Surely you do not believe that?' snorted the inspector.

'It's all a question of perspective. Is it not?'

Sitting in the stuffy interview room, John Blizzard thought of his unborn child, thought of the years ahead, thought of the dangers, thought of the concerns and the anxieties to come, and knew, knew in that moment like no other, that whatever the future held he was ready to be a father.

'Then it all changed,' said Henry Gallen, calmer now that the tears had subsided. 'According to the diary, she got very drunk at the party. She wasn't a big drinker, wasn't Amy, and they just kept pouring it down her throat.'

'Was she drunk enough to know what was happening to her?' asked Blizzard.

'She said it was all pretty vague. What she did remember was at the end of the night, she started to head back; she had been living in one of the chalets. She was the only one left at that stage, the others had gone. Just her and the three men.'

'Exactly what happened?' asked Blizzard, not sure that he wanted to hear the details.

'She only had a hazy memory of it, like I said, but she had a vague recollection of one of them grabbing her as she tried to get out of the door.'

'It was Rawcliffe who grabbed her,' said Heavens. 'The kid was on her way out and he tried to fondle her breasts.'

'And you did nothing to stop him?' said Blizzard, struggling to control his revulsion. 'You knew what George Rawcliffe was like yet you did nothing to stop him?'

'I didn't touch her, though, I would never—'

'For fuck's sake, Jason, that's no—'

'Did Rawcliffe rape her?' interrupted Colley, noting the DCI's furious demeanour, shooting him a warning look and taking over the questioning.

'I don't know.' Heavens saw Colley's sceptical expression. 'Honestly, I don't know. He and Smart took her upstairs into the office. She did not seem to resist, so if they did have sex I'm not sure you'd call it rape. It's such an ugly word, isn't it?'

Blizzard looked away and started to count to ten.

'Was she raped?' asked Colley.

'I don't know,' said Gallen quietly. 'The diary doesn't say if she was. She was probably so drunk she wouldn't know anyway.'

'How come she was still there a week later? Why the hell did she not get away when she could?'

'Do you think I have not asked myself that question a thousand times?' said Gallen. 'I wake up in the middle of the night and the question is always there. Why? Why?'

'And what's the answer?

'Like I said, she wanted the money. She had a week left until her contract finished and the owners had gone so clearly she thought she was safe. Apparently, the party was the only time they'd been there during the whole season. There was only her left by this time, cleaning the place after the season had finished. The diary says that fragments of memory started to come back as the days passed and she began to realize that something terrible had happened to her.'

'But even then she never reported it?' asked Colley.

'She was very private, was Amy, and she knew Mum would kill her if she found out what she'd been up to. Mum was a very moral woman, teetotal, big churchgoer, and she would have been furious if she knew her daughter had been drinking.'

'But there was no way your mother could have blamed Amy for what happened, surely?' said the sergeant.

'I'm not sure Amy would have seen it that way. My mother was a very judgemental woman. I think my sister hoped it would all go away.'

'So what happened the day she died?' a calmer Blizzard asked Heavens,

'I was not there.'

'Yes, but—'

'So I don't know.' Heavens folded his arms if the conversation was at an end.

'Come on,' said Blizzard. 'You know all right.'

'OK, OK, but it was nothing to do with me, right? Rawcliffe grew increasingly worried that the kid would go to the police. Or tell her family. He and Smart went down there, told everyone they were going to a business meeting but they went to the chalet park. They knew she'd be on her own. Next thing I heard she was dead.'

'So you think they killed her?'

'By my reckoning, the only people who can tell you the answer to that are dead. The local police certainly didn't turn up anything.'

'There was a police investigation,' said Blizzard, looking at Gallen. 'How come it did not find the diary?'

'It was hidden in a compartment in her case. I don't think the cops were really looking, to be honest. There was nothing to suggest it was anything other than an accident, was there? The party was a week before and none of the other girls said anything, didn't want their parents to know what they'd been up to, I guess. And Amy *was* on her own when she died. It was case closed as far as the police were concerned.'

'But not for you,' said Blizzard. 'You decided they were guilty, didn't you, Henry?'

Gallen gave a slight smile. 'Everyone's guilty of something,' he said. 'Isn't that what you always say, Chief Inspector?'

'It's not always that simple.'

'It is for me.'

'One last thing before we finish, Jason,' said Blizzard. 'Why come back to Hafton? I mean, why take the risk when you must have known that Henry Gallen had killed the others?'

'I had no option. He said if I didn't tell him what happened to his sister, he'd hack into my bank accounts and steal all the money.' Heavens gave one of his smiles. 'At the end of the day, everything comes down to money, does it not, Chief Inspector?'

'So it would seem,' said Blizzard, standing up and leaving the room.

An hour later, Blizzard was back in the interview room where he and DC Jeffers looked across the table at Roy Meehan and his solicitor.

'You can't prove that I helped Henry Gallen steal anything, you know,' said the professor. He seemed more confident now following the shock of his arrest. 'You have nothing on me.'

'Yes, our forensics team said that you'd been a busy boy with the shredder,' said the inspector.

Meehan met his gaze calmly. 'So can I go?' he said.

'Not just yet. You see, Professor, I have learned so much during this investigation, it really has been quite an eye-opener for an old dinosaur like me. For a start, however careful you might think you've been there's always something called, what is it you people call it again, a digital trail? Is that the phrase?'

Meehan looked anxious.

'Then to compound things you opened up a bank account in a fake name, did you not?' said Blizzard. 'Now why on earth would you do that?'

Meehan closed his eyes.

'With Eastern Counties, oddly enough,' continued the inspector, reaching for the brown file lying on the desk and producing a series of bank statements. 'And when they found out what you had been doing, they were only too happy to help with our inquiry. Funny that, isn't it?' He glanced at the top paper. 'My, my, lecturers do get paid a lot, don't they? I'm in the wrong job.'

Shortly after 8 p.m., the inspector was sitting in his office, letting the weariness wash over him, when Colley walked in, carrying several brown files.

'Think that just about wraps things up,' said the sergeant, sitting down and placing the files on the large pile of papers on the desk. 'I've told Fothergill that, since the only person who can prove that he made the threatening phone calls is dead, we'll let him go as long as he brings his knock-off telly in. Don't want to add to the paperwork, do we?'

Blizzard looked at the documents on his desk and shook his head.

'It'll take ages to sort this little lot out as it is.' He